Connor's Saga

Rocky Mountain Series Book 4

Kurt James

DEDICATION

To my granddaughters Connor & Keegan, for it is through them that I am immortal. Love you both more than you will ever know.

Kurt James

ACKNOWLEDGMENTS

Without the help from my good friend Kurt "Wally" Wollenweber, I would never be able to follow my dream of being a storyteller.
I would also like to thank my friend Brent Lehner for his help in fine tuning this story.

Disclaimer

This is a work of fiction. Names, characters, businesses, places, events and incidents are either the products of the author's imagination or used in a fictitious manner. Any resemblance to actual persons, living or dead, or actual events is purely coincidental.

Kurt James

Kurt James

TABLE OF CONTENTS

Chapter 1

Finding the hidden entrance to the valley known as Redemption Valley had been pure luck. Seeing the bull elk suddenly vanish as it moved silently through the evergreen and aspen trees, I was led to the game trail that finally gave up the entrance to this veiled valley. Spending the last full day searching below timberline on Boreas Pass, Colorado had been frustrating since time was of the essence. The man I was seeking and whom I believed lived within the confines of Redemption Valley would not want any visitors from the outside. The man known as "Ghost" to the Ute Indians of these mountains was as capable and dangerous as any man or foe that ever walked the Rocky Mountain frontier. There was no doubt he would not be happy to see me and any reunion could prove deadly.

Palming my Colt, I made sure it was loaded with a full complement of six. Sliding the pistol quietly back into the holster, I left the leather thong off the hammer that kept it from falling out while riding. I was riding into unknown territory and more than likely danger and I needed my weapons to be ready. For the first quarter of a mile, I was riding through a natural sluice in the shape of "V" and was the most perfect ambush site I had ever seen. Even on this chilly autumn day, the sweat beaded on my forehead, and I thought to myself, "Eric Robert, you are getting too old for this shit!"

My newly acquired mare Gypsy was a tad anxious trailing through such a narrow gap as if she understood the possibility of jeopardy within the hidden valley. Gypsy was a Gidran Arabian and a rare breed first bred in Hungary in the early 1800's. The Gidran's are known for their speed, stamina, agility, and courage. Gypsy like most Gidran's has a smaller head and a straight profile with well-shaped crest and small ears. My Gypsy girl is sixteen hands tall and a very muscular and powerful horse. To the best of my knowledge, all the Gidran's were chestnut in color and Gypsy was no exception. She did however have two rear white socks that were the only breakup of her being a total chestnut color. Since I had bought her three months ago at a horse auction in Denver, we have bonded and had gotten used to each other. Gypsy's intelligence was exceptional, and it helped that her eyesight, hearing, and sense of smell were better than any other horse I have ever owned. When Gypsy was a tad nervous, it made me nervy as well.

Moving almost silently, Gypsy and I made the end of the natural sluice which brought us into a wider valley surrounded by mountains in a bowl shape. The mountains towered on all sides to the point of stretching above timberline. Each mountain, due to its lofty height, had a topping of snow that never melted even during the summer months. Bringing Gypsy to a halt, I surveyed all before me.

If this was Redemption Valley and home of Matt Lee, the man the Ute Indians called "Ghost" and his wife Walk With Ghost, I could see why they chose to live here. It was simple really; the splendor took my breath away. In this hidden valley, they could be free of all the Indian hatred of the white man and those that wanted to see Matt Lee hanged for killing several members of the Colorado 3rd Calvary that had assaulted Walk With Ghost last year in Grand Lake, Colorado.

The golden leaves of autumn of the aspen trees were in full swing here in this obscure valley foretold of the cold and snow that was not far off of the winter months. Looking at the game trail below Gypsy's feet, I could only see deer, elk, and a few rabbits that had used it in recent times. There were no footprints of man nor horse which meant if Matt Lee and Walk With Ghost were within the valley, they had not used this trail to leave since the last rain. After taking a long swig of cool water from my canteen, I gave Gypsy her head and the reins, and we moved forward cautiously into the Ghost lair.

Following the game trail and the flight of a red-tailed hawk as it flew overhead, Gypsy and I saw no movement of any kind other than the slight wind that was causing the aspen leaves to quake. The only sound was that of the saddle creaking and that of the woods, nothing out of the ordinary.

The center of Redemption Valley had a small stream that flowed west to east as it meandered lazily across the valley floor, supplying fresh water to all that lived here within these walls. Scanning the tree lines and hoping to see any telltale sign of Matt Lee and his wife who lived here amongst the wilderness, I saw none, so Gypsy and I moved forward as silently as possible.

Searching for Matt Lee had been a last-minute choice on my part, and I was now doubting the wisdom of that decision. So many misgivings and thoughts crossed my mind now. First, this might not be Redemption Valley at all. Second, if in fact this was Redemption Valley, Matt Lee and Walk With Ghost may have changed their minds and decided to hide elsewhere from the law and those that wanted the man named Ghost dead. Third, my real mission was being delayed by searching for Matt Lee the famous mountain man. This could all end up being a wasted folly on my part, and time was not on my side.

Following the stream further into the valley, I finally cut a trail that headed to the south. Stopping Gypsy, I stepped out of the saddle and with bent knees, I studied the game trail as it meandered in between the evergreens and aspens to the south. There had been recent activity on this trail of not only elk and deer, but also that of a shod horse heading south. A big and powerful horse, in fact, much like the one I last saw Matt Lee riding on

Kenosha Pass over a year ago. Looking down the trail, I knew it was a big risk in heading that way.

Once again the sweat beaded on my forehead in anticipation of what lay ahead. I palmed my Colt once again just to see if the dampness of this autumn day had not made it stick to my leather holster. The pistol slid easily into my hand, which I hoped was not a false feeling of security. The mountain man known as Ghost was as deadly of a foe that has ever ridden the timberline.

After placing my Colt back into the holster on my right side, I then pulled my Winchester rifle from the scabbard hanging on Gypsy and jacked a shell into the firing chamber. The sound of levering a shell startled me in the silence of the woods as it echoed off the high walls of the valley. Dumb! Real dumb, Eric Robert!

I stood still trying to gather in all that was surrounding me hoping the sound of my rifle was not my undoing. There was no movement, and I felt the loneliness of the woods. I knew full well that Matt Lee had the skill set that would not let his presence be known until he was upon me. He had not survived all these years by being sloppy in his woodcraft when so many wanted his hair. Matt Lee had survived an all-out war against the Ute Indians, US Calvary pursuit, bounty hunters, and myself in the years past.

Sliding the Winchester silently back into the scabbard and then after squaring my butt in the saddle and then giving Gypsy some rein and her head, we moved out.

After a quarter of a mile next to the stream, I saw something I did not expect to see - a simple wooden cross marking a freshly dug grave. My heart dropped as I dismounted Gypsy to get closer to read the inscription on the marker. The words that had been recently carved were easily read, "Walk With Ghost - Ute Indian princess and my wife. Not a day went by that I didn't love her."

My heart sank, for I had known Walk With Ghost for only a short while and she was one hell of a woman that is for sure. She, even in her later years, was a beautiful woman with the grace of a queen. She always stood by her man Ghost when push came to shove, and their love for one another was unmatched by any other couple I had ever known. Matt Lee always claimed his wife was the only thing that kept him sane after what happened those many years ago on Marble Mountain at the La Caverna Del Oro. The legend of "Ghost" began over forty years ago when Matt Lee had been the sole survivor of a Ute Indian massacre of his friends. The death of his wife could have sent him back over the edge of sanity. I was not so sure now was a good time to be pursuing the man and the legend named Ghost.

Standing up and still looking at the grave marker, I felt the cold steel of a pistol barrel as it touched the back of my head. Closing my eyes and waiting for the outcome, I heard a voice I had not heard in over a year. It was obvious that Matt Lee had ghosted up on me. Speaking in a calm and clear voice, Matt Lee said, "Marshal Eric Robert, what brings you to my valley?"

Chapter 2

Not wanting to move suddenly, I replied in a calm voice, "Sorry about Walk With Ghost. I truly am. She was a good woman to put up with your shenanigans all these years. I cannot imagine how difficult it was to live with a man such as yourself."

I heard the click of the hammer of the pistol that was touching the back of my head and as it was being pulled back, a bead of sweat broke out on my forehead. There was silence for a full minute before Matt Lee spoke again. "Do you remember the time in Grand Lake when you had a pistol pointed at my head, Eric Robert?"

Not sure where this was headed, I spoke again with more calm than I was feeling. "I do Matt Lee. I also remember shortly after that you had a gun pointed at my head. So if we are keeping count, you are winning two to one in that department."

I felt the pressure on the back of my head disappear as Matt Lee released the hammer slowly and holstered his Colt as he chuckled softly and said, "I reckon I am, Marshal. You want some coffee?

Mine is not as good as Walk With Ghost used to make. In fact, you could stand a horseshoe straight up in it, but it is all I have and you are welcome to it."

As I turned to face the man I hunted almost a year ago, Matt Lee the famous mountain man looked just as I remembered him. The legend was 6' 2" tall with shoulder length pure white hair due to his advanced years, and he had piercing and intelligent brown eyes. I did not know his age, but he had to be well past sixty years old. His body was still lean and strong, and he still moved with grace and agility as he walked into the timber in front of me. He was a man accustomed to living life as he saw fit, regardless of the outcome. I hunted him when my job warranted it, but he never was my enemy. Last time I saw him on Kenosha Pass, we rode in different directions, not as the law and the wanted man, but with an understanding of friendship. After seeing him now in his hidden valley, it felt good to see him. I missed our talks we had before and after what had happened on the streets of Grand Lake, Colorado when a Union soldier had tried to kill his wife.

While walking behind Matt Lee and while holding the reins of Gypsy who trailed behind me, I thought about how I would stack up against someone such as Matt Lee in hand-to-hand combat if this encounter with the legend went south. We both were about the same age and size, weighing in at about 190 pounds or so. My hair was short and gray and the weeks' worth of stubble on my chin was pure white. My eyes were brown just like the legend's eyes, but not as piercing as his were. I still had strength in my arms and legs, but not like I used to in my youth. All in all I think it would be a wash if it ever came to a fistfight between the two of us. Something I would rather not see.

We walked almost silently through the dense evergreen and aspen trees, and it was not long before I could smell wood smoke from the direction we were traveling. Gypsy tugged hard on the reins as I held her and looking back, I could see tension mounting in her eyes as she was staring into the woods. Something or someone was out there behind the trees. Out of the corner of my eye, I saw movement on my right - a slash of white fur, but too far into the woods for me to get a good look. Stopping and trying to calm Gypsy, I glared into the woods trying to see what was there. Finally, I focused in on a pair of yellow eyes of an almost pure white wolf. I palmed my Colt to arm myself and ready myself to take action against the wolf if needed. Matt Lee had also stopped and had seen my actions, and he also had seen the wolf as well. Speaking in an almost nonchalant way, he said, "Holster your weapon, Marshal; that is just Timber."

After I looked at the wolf who still was not advancing and then back at Matt Lee, I replied, "Timber? You know what you are calling Timber is a wolf, Matt Lee?"

Matt Lee chuckled once again and said, "Glad to see your eyes have not gotten sour for you in your old age, Marshal. Timber is not looking for a meal just yet. He ate a whole turkey just this morning. I suggest you put the gun away before Timber starts to take a disliking to you."

Warily and after holstering my weapon, I turned back to the white as snow wolf as he moved in closer as if he needed to check out Gypsy and myself. What the hell! Matt Lee has a tamed wolf! Just as that thought crossed my mind, Matt Lee spoke a word of caution. "I warn you do not go to thinking Timber is tame because he is not. He comes and goes as he pleases and fends for himself in the hunting of his own food. The only person who could pet him was Walk With Ghost. Timber is not as trusting of me in that regard. He is no threat to you or your horse as long as you make no move to harm him. I have warned you, and I will not warn you a second time."

Timber moved in until he was on my side of the tree line, but he stopped short of Gypsy and me by twenty feet and just sat down, studying us. I had seen wolves before in my lifetime and even hunted a few for the bounty, but I had never seen one that was pure white before. Timber was huge, probably about 160 pounds and heavily muscled. His eyes were yellow, which I had never seen before in such a magnificent animal. He was not threatening nor was the wolf friendly. Timber's intelligence showed through his eyes as he sat silently studying me. It was obvious the only reason he tolerated me was because I was with Matt Lee. I hate to think what Timber could do if he took a sudden disapproving of me.

Cautiously I took my eyes off the white wolf and looked to Gypsy, calmed considerably sensing that the wolf was no threat. Gypsy, like me, gingerly followed Matt Lee as he headed inward into the hidden valley. Timber the wolf's curiosity must have been satisfied as he faded back into the tree line.

It was not long until we followed the trail out of the evergreens and aspens into a small meadow. In the middle of the meadow stood a small cabin with smoke rising from the chimney. Next to the wood cabin stood a rude, but fairly large corral that had two horses in it. Both horses I knew from before.

Spirit, a mare, used to be a Ute Indian war pony that Matt Lee had won in an arm wrestling contest. She was a big horse at almost eighteen hands tall and was chestnut in color except for her right front leg, which had a pure white sock that stretched all the way to her knee. I remember her to be an intelligent horse. The other horse was almost as famous as Matt Lee himself.

Cimarron, an Appaloosa Gruella mare, once had been owned by the equally famous bounty hunter Doug Webb. Webb had trailed after Matt Lee for the $2000 bounty that had been placed on his head. The bounty and arrest warrant came to be when Matt Lee avenged the shooting of his wife in Grand Lake by killing the four soldiers that had assaulted Walk With Ghost. In a twist of fate, I had actually killed Doug Webb just as he was getting ready to kill Matt Lee after a savage fight on top of Kenosha Pass near the South Platte River. Cimarron was grayish with white spots over her back and hips. Her facial markings comprised a white as snow star in between the eyes and a white snip below the top of the nostrils. And her hind legs both had partial white socks. And she had the mottled skin around her mouth and the Appaloosa trait of striped hooves. What set her aside from other Appaloosa mares was she was bigger than most at almost nineteen hands tall and heavily muscled with stamina second to none. The story goes that once she rode at a fast trot for two days straight without tiring or floundering. Cimarron was also a man killer having killed two men on two different occasions that had tried to steal her from the now deceased bounty hunter by kicking them to death. Cimarron now belonged to Matt Lee.

There was a hitching rail in front and I tied off Gypsy before following Matt Lee inside of his home. Matt Lee pointed to a wooden rough-hewn chair by a table that looked to have been made by the same hands that had built the chair. The smell of coffee was strong as was the smell of the venison stew that was warming over the fire in the fireplace. The inside of the one-room cabin was neat and tidy, and I could still feel the presence of Walk With Ghost within the walls. Even with never having been in this home, it felt empty because Walk With Ghost was not there. Matt Lee's and the Ute princess' love for one another was what the poets always wrote about. In my short time with them over a year ago, I felt the romance, and I envied them for it. It was one of the reasons I did what I had done in letting them go. It was a decision I never regretted.

Matt Lee without talking set a steaming bowl of venison stew and a hot cup of coffee in front of me. He did likewise for himself on the other side of the table. Once he settled into his chair, I finally asked what was begging to be asked, "What happened regarding Walk With Ghost?"

Matt Lee stopped and put his cup of coffee down and looked me in the eye for a spell as he gathered his thoughts. A tear formed in his eye as he spoke. "She caught the fever two weeks ago, and no matter how hard I tried or how much I prayed, the Good Lord decided he needed another angel. In the last few days since I buried her, I have pondered the meaning of our lives together and the more than forty years we spent with one another. I have decided that grief is the price we pay for loving someone when they die. This price I would have willingly paid just to be with her. It honored me that she chose me to spend her life with. As you know in so many ways it was she that saved me from myself. Walk With Ghost was my lover and best friend, and she was one to ride the river with. My whole life with her was about keeping her safe from all those that would wish her harm just because she was a Ute Indian. Not sure what I will do without her; I never gave it much thought I guess. I always thought with the life I have led that it would be me that died first. There is a hole in my heart, Eric Robert and by God I miss her so!"

I sat in silence not knowing what to say, for I could feel Matt Lee's pain as if it was my own. "Now I am not sure, Eric Robert what just got into me; that was more words than I have spoken to another white man in nearly ten years. Please forgive me for being rude. Now Marshal, you did not track me down for a cup of coffee and there is no way in hell you could have known of Walk With Ghost's dire sickness. So what in the hell are you doing here?"

Chapter 3

While looking Matt Lee straight in the eye, I said, "I know this comes at a bad time Matt Lee, but I need your help!"

Matt Lee set his coffee cup down gently and then remarked, "After you released me from custody on Kenosha Pass and let me spend the rest of Walk With Ghost's life with her in relative harmony, I reckon I owe you. So tell me what this old mountain man can do for you, Marshal Robert."

I knew full well that what would come next would put both Matt Lee's life and my life in harm's way. Clearing my voice, I told him the reason. "My ten year old granddaughter Connor has been kidnapped and is being held for ransom. I intend to go fetch her and kill the son of a bitch that kidnapped her."

Matt Lee's eyebrow lifted a tad before he spoke, "Ransom?"

It was difficult for me to ask for help when it came to a family matter, but Connor's kidnapping was not your normal day family matter. With what was facing me down the trail, I would need help from someone that could be ruthless and deadly. Matt Lee fits that description, and he needed to know what he was getting involved with. Clearing my throat before I answered, "Yes a $100,000 ransom. Have you ever heard of the Scottish bandit Alistair McPherson and his brother Alban?"

Matt Lee's eyes widened when he heard the name, and then he spoke, "Yes, I have, thinking everyone west of Missouri has heard of the Highlander bandits. The story goes they had to flee Scotland when the older Alistair killed with a knife two men who had teased his younger brother Alban. After reaching America, they became road agents and thieves and robbed and murdered their way west. Some say the Highlanders steal women and sell them down south to Mexican bandits. Along with his excellent knife skills, they say Alistair is also a quick draw on the par with Lucas Eldridge, Chance Bondurant, and even Johnny Ringo. I had not heard they were in Colorado though."

It would seem the Highlanders' reputation had even made tracks beyond the walls of this hidden valley. After a swig of Matt Lee's awful tasting coffee, I continued, "About six months ago, they showed up in Victor and Cripple Creek, Colorado. Alistair McPherson, his brother, and their gang of roughly ten to twelve hard cases and cutthroats are said to have taken up refuge in Phantom Canyon and making it their headquarters. The mouth of Phantom Canyon is two miles south of Victor which puts them within a day's ride of the rich gold camps there. They have been robbing the stagecoaches and stealing from the independent gold miners. The local law has been unable to cope with the situation down there. Roughly three months ago Alistair McPherson kidnapped the granddaughter of W.S. Stratton the owner of the Independence Mine near Cripple Creek and demanded a ransom of $100,000. Stratton paid the ransom, but the Highlanders took the girl south with a few other young girls they had kidnapped and sold them like you say to some Mexican bandits. As long as there is still life in this old body, he will not do that to my Connor."

After saying my piece, I pushed the coffee cup away and pulled the bowl of stew closer, hoping Matt Lee couldn't screw up venison stew as badly as he had the coffee. Matt Lee had already begun eating his stew, and he stopped spooning into his mouth after I had finished and looked as if he was pondering what I had said before he spoke. "I got two questions. Do you or your family have $100,000? And if not, why would the Highlanders think you had that kind of money to pay the ransom?"

"My family does not, but my daughter Jessica married well. Jessica married an Irishman named Brody O'Brien, who is Connor's father. Brody's father is Finn O'Brien who happens to own the London and Mosquito Mines on top of Mosquito Pass south of Alma, Colorado. It would seem that the O'Brien family has done well or at least the Highlanders think they are well off. The ransom demand was directed at them."

Matt Lee was quiet as he finished his bowl of stew, and I wondered if he was going to decline going with me. If the aging mountain man stayed here, then it had been a waste of my time coming here. Since time was of the essence, I was getting a tad perturbed not at Matt Lee, but at myself. I needed to get on the trail because Connor's life hung in the balance. Not being a patient man regarding waiting until someone makes up his mind, I asked, "Well, Ghost, is it yes or no?"

Matt Lee set his empty bowl aside and looked me square in the eye and said, "My thought is if I don't go, you will probably get yourself killed by these Scottish outlaws. Even if Walk With Ghost was still alive, she would want me to go. She liked you and always told me how much of a good man you were for doing the righteous thing a year ago on Kenosha Pass. So, yes, I will go with you to fetch your granddaughter. Do you want more coffee?"

It relieved me to have someone who had the skills that Matt Lee did by my side and watching my back. I thought now it was not wasted time coming here and that I just doubled Connor's chances of being rescued. With a smile on my face and in a clear voice, "Much appreciated, Matt Lee. Wondering, if I say your coffee is just about as rank as I have ever drunk, would that change your mind?"

Matt Lee stood up and took my coffee cup and tossed the sour tasting black water into the fireplace, and he said with a smirk, "Well, Marshal that is about the most honest thing you could have ever said. Never was much of a coffee maker. It will be dark in an hour and I suggest we leave in the morning. There is an old cranky brown bear I share this valley with, and I do not believe you and I want to meet him on the trail in the dark. So you best eat more stew and unsaddle your horse and bring your bedroll in for the night."

I did not really want to waste any more time, but I could see the wisdom of Matt Lee's words. It would not benefit Connor if I got maimed or killed by a cranky bear tonight at the beginning of this bid to rescue her. Deciding I would take care of Gypsy first before having another bowl of tasty stew, I walked out the door of the cabin. After taking the saddle of Gypsy just before I turned her into the corral with Spirit and Cimarron, I gave her a good currying with a wooden brush I carried in my saddlebags. After giving Gypsy some sugar for a treat, I let her loose in the corral to get herself familiar with the other horses. In the next couple of weeks, they would spend a lot of time with each other.

After the chore of taking care of Gypsy, I leaned on the corral fence and watched the autumn sun finish its arc down below the mountains to the west. In my mind, there was nothing more full of grandeur than a Rocky Mountain sunset in all of its orange glory. It always seemed that the colors stood out more in the autumn and winter months. The wind had picked up slightly, and a few golden aspen leaves were doing a dance on its current. As soon as the sun dropped below the horizon, the air chilled and reminded me that the first snows of the winter were not far off. My aging bones would protest the onslaught of winter tomorrow morning. Growing old was not a pleasant affair.

Once back inside the cabin, I used the ladle to scoop up another bowl of stew. Matt Lee was keeping busy cleaning his Colt pistol and Winchester rifle. His bowie knife was lying on the table, and it was clear he had just sharpened it as well. Matt Lee, the man known as "Ghost," was - when necessary - a killer, bar none. He was exactly what I needed! He was exactly what Connor needed right now.

As soon as Matt Lee was done cleaning his weapons, he went to the cabin door and opened it. He wet his lips and with a loud whistle that annoyed my ears, he let loose and whistled into the night. Not more than a minute passed, and Timber the white wolf came trotting through the door and found what seemed to be an all familiar spot by the fire to lie down.

As soon as Timber had lain down, Matt turned and said, "Don't feed him any stew. I will not have him coddled. He fends for himself."

I did not want to point out to a man that in his time had brought death to over twenty of the best Ute warriors in hand-to-hand combat that letting the mysterious white wolf in to enjoy the fire was coddling the beast. Chuckling, I replied, "I would not even think of it, Matt Lee."

The cabin was warm and sleep was coming easy as I lay on the floor near Timber who was now in a deep sleep and snoring. Matt Lee was still awake, and his voice came out of the darkness and the dancing light of the flames of the fire. "What does Connor look like? Just in case we get separated or you get killed, I need to know who to look for. She might be mixed in with some other young girls."

That was a good question and one I had no answer for. Replying to my new partner, "I was never a good father to Jessica. I was always on the trail doing my job and never spent much time at home. I cannot remember the last time I spoke to my daughter other than the telegram she sent me in Denver last week. That is why we have to go to Alma, Colorado first to speak to my daughter and second to get a photograph of Connor. In her ten young years, I have never seen my granddaughter. I have no idea what she looks like."

Chapter 4

The next morning before sunrise and after a cold breakfast of jerky and hardtack biscuits, we made ready for the trail. I saddled Gypsy, and Matt Lee made Spirit and Cimarron ready. The aging mountain man had packed away his buckskin shirt and breeches and wore some Levi jeans and a flannel shirt and a knee-length black duster. I was sporting the same except my duster was tan. On our heads we both wore older cattleman crease Stetsons that had seen better days. Mine was tan to match my duster, and Matt Lee's was black. Each of us carried a twelve inch Bowie knife on our left side and a Colt pistol on our right hip with the grip facing backwards in a standard draw. Matt Lee had one scabbard with his Winchester 44 housed inside as did I. I also carried a second scabbard that had a loaded twelve gauge Greener shotgun for close-up work - the same one I had killed the bounty hunter Webb with.

Once we were squared into our saddles, Timber, the white wolf with the yellow eyes, emerged from the evergreens to the west and stopped and planted his butt not ten feet away from Matt Lee and Cimarron. Matt Lee and the wolf stared at one another for a full minute before Matt Lee spoke, "Timber, the place is yours if you want it or you can tag along if you desire. We can't lollygag around here waiting for you to make up your mind. So what will it be my four-legged friend?"

Timber stood and wagged his tail just as a normal dog would, and then he howled for a second or two. Matt Lee looked at me and said, "Guess it is settled then. He is going with."

Shaking my head wondering what the hell we would do with a wolf on the trail, I simply replied, "I reckon so."

The sun was just peeking above the mountain to the east as we started to make our way out of the hidden valley that Matt Lee and Walk With Ghost had named Redemption Valley. The air was chilly, and the wind had a bite to it this morning as it rustled the leaves enough for them to sing their dying song of autumn.

As we came up on Walk With Ghost's grave, Matt Lee reined Cimarron in that direction and then he dismounted. Out of respect for the aging mountain man and his love for his departed wife, I kept my distance. Matt Lee kneeled on one knee in front of the wooden cross, and I could see his lips moving as he spoke to his wife. I was far enough away that I could not hear his words, but the sag of his shoulders spoke of the grief he was feeling. My heart ached for the mountain man. I knew his love was genuine since I had seen it for myself. I envied him in his loss, for I had no wife in my life over whom I could grieve. My one and only wife and the grandmother of Connor had left me for a store clerk so many years ago I had lost count. I had no ill feelings toward my wife since I was a rotten husband, and she deserved better than a lawman that was never home.

After saying what he needed to say, Matt Lee mounted up and trotted past me saying, "Let's go, Eric Robert and get your granddaughter."

Once we had made it out of the hidden valley, I turned to Matt Lee and told him that I thought that the town of Alma was sixteen or seventeen miles and we should make it easily this day. I reined Gypsy in the general direction of Como which was the first town of many that we would ride through or near that was on our trail.

Timber was staying by Matt Lee's side as he rode and looked as if he would not have any problem with keeping up with the horses. I still did not know what to think of the white wolf with yellow eyes and if he would be a hindrance in my quest to free my granddaughter or not. One thing for sure though, Timber seemed to be enjoying the outing.

As we rode just on the outskirts of Como, I pondered all that I knew about the town. Como was not only a coal mining town but also was an important hub for the surrounding gold camps on both sides of the Great Divide. It had a roundhouse so they could turn the railroad engines around and then head them back up over Boreas Pass. Como was named after Como, Italy since most of the coal miners had come from there. Como also was a town that had in recent years some famous gunfights happen right there on its streets. Lucas Eldridge, who was like a son to Matt Lee, had fought and killed the gunfighters Rick Pryce and Irish Bob O'Connor for kidnapping and beating his soon to be wife Devin. Just recently the former Confederate soldier McCall Patton, known as Rebel Mac, had shot and killed the former Union Captain John Merna, John Loveless, and the gunfighter Larry Brown, who had been known as LB in the now famous gun battle that had been fought on the main street of Como. We had plenty of supplies so we would not be stopping in the mining settlement on this day.

By mid-morning with the sun warming the earth, we stopped at Trout Creek and let the horses and Timber get their fill of cool creek water. Once that was done, we pushed on west toward Alma. Drinking my fill from my canteen and thinking of what was coming, I got nervy about seeing my daughter Jessica. It had been so long since I had seen her it worried me that I might not recognize her. There was no doubt I loved my daughter, but I had never been the father that I should have been to my one and only child. My job as a federal marshal took me away from home in Denver so much that being a good father had been out of the question. In the early years, being on the trail and tracking down outlaws seemed the correct course of action to take, and I believed I was doing right by my wife and daughter. During those long ago days, doing my job and doing it right was all that mattered and in my mind it was how it was supposed to be. Now in my later years, I realize that was not the case, and I had regrets. In some ways I hoped if I could rescue Connor that it might heal some heartache of my relationship with Jessica.

By midday we cut across the trail that headed south six or seven miles into the town of Fairplay. Just like most of the towns scattered along the Rocky Mountain frontier, Fairplay was a rough and tumble town born in the early days of the Pikes Peak gold rush. Fairplay also happened to be the largest settlement in the high mountain plateau of what was called South Park. This high mountain flat land, which we were now trailing through, was one of three Rocky Mountain wonders. North Park, Middle Park, and South Park were mountain grassland flats spread north to south in the Rocky Mountains of Colorado. South Park was roughly 1000 square miles of flat land which was just a tad below timberline. Riding through South Park, I got a sense of how small and trivial I was in these mountains of old; the surrounding mountain tops were forever white with the snows that never melt at those lofty heights. It was my belief that the Lord made the world but saved the Rocky Mountains for his last and his best work. The majestic grandeur I lived and worked in was breathtaking to say the least.

The sun by mid-afternoon had already started its downward arc toward the western horizon as Matt Lee and I rode in silence as two men of the mountains do. Not engaging in unnecessary talk was part of who we were. Matt Lee finally asked a question when we stopped to water the horses at Beaver Creek. "I see, Marshal you are not wearing your badge and I wonder why that is?"

Dismounting, I pulled a half pound of deer jerky from my saddlebag for a quick meal before replying, "You know why Matt Lee? What is at the end of this trail is not for the law to handle. I am not riding to rescue my granddaughter as a lawman; I am riding as a grandfather to right a wrong that was inflicted on my family. I plan on killing the Scottish outlaw, his brother, and any other son of a bitch that gets in my way. It is as simple as that. My badge has no place in what I am planning to do."

Matt Lee had watched me as I answered his question with his all-knowing eyes. "Well, I reckon I have never been much for taking prisoners myself. We will get your granddaughter back or we will die trying."

As the sun slowly faded, and the day became night, we camped a mile away from Alma not wanting to ride into an unfamiliar town in the darkness. It was best to study the settlement in daylight for a spell and get the lay of the land. Men born of the mountains were never in a hurry; being in a hurry gets you killed. Matt Lee and I didn't get to be our age by rushing things.

Matt and I took considerable time to care for the horses before tending to ourselves, as it should be. Without a good horse, a man is nothing in regard to what the mountains can throw at you. The horses always come first.

The air chilled considerably as the man known as Ghost and I started our supper of fat backed bacon and fried beans. Once we had our supper fixings on tin plates, Timber faded into the now darkened forest of evergreens and aspens looking for his evening meal I suspected. The white wolf so far was almost pleasant to have on the trail with us. It would seem he was here to stay.

Looking at the cloudless sky and the heavens filled with shiny and twinkling stars, I thought of what was to come. Tomorrow I will ride to Alma and face my daughter. I was nervous as hell.

Chapter 5

Timber woke both Matt Lee and me several hours before dawn. He didn't howl or growl; he just stood and attentively watched the woods to our west. The white wolf's movement wasn't much, but just enough to break the stillness of the night and to wake the famous mountain man and myself. Matt Lee and I both silently armed ourselves with our Colts and watched not only the wolf but also the horses for any more signs that danger was near. The yellow-eyed wolf with his keen senses would be put to the test more often than not as we got closer to Phantom Canyon and the Scottish outlaws that had kidnapped my granddaughter. I was starting to see the benefit of having Timber along with us. After about a half-hour, Timber relaxed and lay back down and fell into a deep slumber. Whatever the wolf had sensed in the darkness had moved on to parts unknown. With hand signals Matt Lee indicated he would see to the horses and that I should start the chore of getting breakfast started. It seemed reasonable to me since there would be no use trying to get more shuteye at this point.

I stirred the embers from last night's cooking fire to get the ones still smoldering deep down in the ashes to the top so the chilled air could reawaken the flames. Having done that, I added kindling, and before long I had a flame dancing a burning jig on the crackle and sizzle of the aspen wood. After Timber had awakened from his slumber, he fetched himself a big plump squirrel for his own breakfast. It was not long before I had fat backed bacon and beans sizzling in the frying pan. After making campfire tortillas, I had the fixing for a mighty fine breakfast for the Ghost and myself.

After we ate breakfast and got the horses ready for the trail, the sun was now lighting the eastern horizon above the mountaintops. There was not a cloud in sight as the stars above faded away. The air still had that autumn night chill to it, so I turned up the collar of my duster to help ward off the dampness and the cold.

Since this was my party, I gave Gypsy some rein and her head as I pointed her in the direction of Alma. Matt Lee, Timber, Spirit, and Cimarron followed.

The sun was now fully up when the Ghost and I stopped short about a quarter of a mile from the mining town of Alma. We stayed back in the evergreen trees as we studied the town for anything that might seem out of kilter. Through my binoculars I could see the settlement was already awake with the townsfolk and miners going here and there taking care of their daily chores. Alma was just like any of the mining towns that sprung up along the Rocky Mountain frontier and had its fill of miners, storekeepers, soiled doves, and I am sure it had more than a few hard cases thrown in. In one regard Alma differed from most of the mining settlements because it was situated just at timberline, which was the line where above it the trees would not grow anymore due to loftier heights. The air was thinner of course here and for a person not born in these mountains, it took a long spell before their lungs would get used to the high mountain air.

From my observation point, I could see the five mountains that were 4000 feet or higher than the settlement of Alma - Mount Sherman, Mount Bross, Mount Lincoln, Mount Democrat, and Mount Cameron. Each of these lordly mountains had a shroud of white snow frosted on top - snow that never melted even in the summer months.

After studying the settlement for about ten minutes, I was able to spot a two-story wood framed building that had a painted sign out front stating that the O'Brien Mining Company was just beyond the front door. After looking at Matt Lee who showed with a nod of his head that his observations were satisfied, I gave Gypsy a slight jab of my spur, and we headed toward the main street of Alma and Jessica. I had my concerns that this meeting with my daughter would not be pleasant.

As we made our way down the dirt road into the town of Alma, everyone on the boardwalks or the thoroughfare turned to watch us. It was not the sight of two heavily armed men and the three horses that made them watch; it was the yellow-eyed wolf that everyone was looking at. Granted, Timber was a magnificent looking animal with his snow white fur, but it was his eyes that held everyone's attention. Timber mostly seemed to enjoy the attention as he walked beside Matt Lee and Cimarron as if he owned the town. Seeing Timber strut with confidence in his first town almost made me laugh.

When we finally made the front of the O'Brien Mining Company door, Timber had a following of young boys and girls that had trailed him as we rode through town. Matt Lee and I both dismounted and Matt said in an annoyed tone, "I better stay here, Marshal to keep Timber's admirers at bay so he doesn't take a hand off one of them if they try to pet him."

Looking at the kids milling around on the boardwalk, I replied, "I reckon that would be best; these miners' offspring don't look like they have much in their brain pans."

Matt Lee chuckled as I stepped up onto the boardwalk and then opened the door to the O'Brien Mining Company. Stopping just inside the door, I saw there was a well-dressed man sitting behind a hardwood desk with an assayer's scale and several leather backed ledgers laying in front of him. The young man was so intent on what he was writing in one ledger that he had not noticed me. Clearing my voice I said, "I was wondering if someone here could help me."

I startled the man at first, and then he stood quickly and after gathering his senses, he asked, "What can I do for you, sir?"

Studying the young man, I wondered if he was my son-in-law and I took several seconds before I replied, "I am looking for

Jessica and Brody O'Brien, and I was hoping someone could point me in their direction."

The young, dark haired man returned my gaze when he spoke loudly, "Jessica, I believe your father is here."

From a room in the building's back without a door, my daughter Jessica stepped through it, and I all but forgot about the young man that stood off to the side. She stood for several minutes, and I was able to get a long look at her. She was stunning with long almost raven colored hair. With her slender figure, she was the spitting image of her mother on the day I married her. The guilt of not being the father I should have been to this young woman that stood before me rushed over me and I felt weak because of it.

Any misgivings that I had on this moment of seeing my daughter for the first time in more years than I could count were dismissed as Jessica flowed into my arms. I held her tight as she was holding me. There was comfort and understanding in our hugs and it felt good. If not for the dire circumstances for why I was here, this moment in my life would have been perfect.

Jessica, who was still holding tightly, separated slightly and looked up with more than a few tears shining her eyes. "Oh Daddy, I knew you would come. Connor, Brody and I needed you and I knew you would come!"

Shedding a few tears of my own, I cleared my voice and said, "Jessica, I will bring back Connor to you or I will die in the attempt. You need to know I will move heaven and earth to make that happen. Since time is a wasting, you need to get me caught up with what happened and what the Highlanders and their gang of cutthroats are asking for exactly."

For the next two hours, I sat in the O'Brien Mining office and heard the tale of my granddaughter's kidnapping and ransom demand. The young man that had been seated at the table when I walked in was my son-in-law Brody. He seemed like a good man and capable enough in a bookish sense but had no wherewithal in terms of having what it would take to track down and engage the men that had stolen his daughter. His father Finn had joined us and was just an older version of his son. Neither of the men would be any help in what needed to be done with the Highlanders.

The task of rescuing Connor would fall on my shoulders; it seemed now that the wisest thing I had done so far since leaving

Denver was to fetch Matt Lee and the wolf Timber. What was waiting for us at the mouth of Phantom Canyon would need men that had grit and a killer instinct. Men that would not hesitate to do what needed to be done and to kill those responsible if the situation warranted it. The lawman inside me had taken a backseat to a grandfather that would serve righteous justice on those that had inflicted pain and suffering on my family.

Finn Brody, Connor's other grandpa, offered to send the $100,000 with me to pay the ransom. Finn, Brody, and Jessica knew the Highlander outlaws could not be trusted after hearing of W.S. Stratton the owner of the Independence mine in Cripple Creek who paid the ransom for his granddaughter and the subsequent betrayal of selling the young lady to Mexican bandits anyway. We all agreed that paying the money was not the answer and that the only course of action was to just take her back. The only thing that the Highlanders would get from me was lead and buckshot.

The priority was to get Connor back safely to Alma and her family. My only concern was that Connor had already been sold to the bandits or even possibly been killed. If either of those things had happened, then there was no limit in what I would do. I would bring a raging storm and ear shattering thunder to Phantom Canyon. The Highlander desperados may not know it yet, but I was bringing Hell to them. Riding alongside me was the specter of death and his name was Matt Lee.

Standing on the boardwalk in front of the O'Brien Mining Company, Jessica gave me a tintype that had the likeness of my granddaughter. Connor looked just like her mother at that age, and it relieved me to know I could pick her out in a crowd of young girls if needed.

Jessica, Brody, and Finn just nodded their heads in acknowledgment after introducing the famous aging mountain man as only Matt. I had to be careful in using the Ghost's real name or even his nickname on the trail. Even though Matt Lee had been thought to have died over a year ago on the top of Kenosha Pass, he still had a bounty of $2000 dollars on his head for the killing of the soldiers that assaulted his wife in Grand Lake. I was the only one that knew the truth about Matt Lee, for it was me who had made it possible for Walk With Ghost and him to fade into the Rocky Mountains.

After a quick handshake for Brody and Finn and a hug and kiss for Jessica, I stepped into the stirrup and mounted Gypsy. Turning to Ghost, who was already mounted, I said to the mountain man, "Are you ready to ride, Matt?"

Ghost gave Spirit a slight jab of his spur while saying, "I reckon so, Marshal. Let's go get your granddaughter and kill us some Scottish assholes!"

Chapter 6

It was mid-morning when we made the town of Fairplay where we stopped and replenished our supplies for the trail. Timber once again was an irresistible attraction for the boys and girls in this town, and he had gathered another following as I ordered and purchased the supplies and as Matt Lee stood guard against any of the more adventurous children that might get too close to the wild wolf and find out he was not tame; however, Timber seemed to be enjoying seeing the children almost as much as they enjoyed seeing him.

The trail was flat and easy through South Park even though its elevation was roughly 9,000 feet. The high mountain grassland was a pleasant trail to ride during the summer and spring but could turn deadly in no time with blowing and drifting snow during the fall and winter. Many of the tinhorns had lost their lives trying to venture across this high mountain plateau in the wrong time of the year after getting caught in a complete whiteout. South Park was scattered with the bones of the not so lucky. Even the caliber of men like Matt Lee and me had fallen victim to the sudden changes of unpredictable weather of South Park. Even though it was now autumn, South Park had not seen its first snowfall as of yet. I hoped to have good weather until Connor was safe.

It was late in the afternoon when we passed through the town of Garo. Garo was nothing to write home about; it was a small town that was founded by a Frenchman named Louis Adolf Guiraud. Louis and his wife Marie also happened to own the largest ranch in the area. The story goes that the town's name was shortened, and a misspelled version of Guiraud; it seems none of the other locals could pronounce Guiraud correctly, hence the misspelling.

Garo sometimes was called a confederate town due to the Frenchman's friendship with the rebel confederate gang known as The Reynolds Gang. John Reynolds and his southern henchmen had operated in these parts at the end of the civil war robbing the gold miners and stages trying to help finance the South in their losing rebellion against ole' Abe Lincoln and the Northern forces. There was a rumor going around that The Reynolds Gang had buried some ill-gotten gains somewhere close to here just before they were captured and subsequently executed. I didn't put much stock in the buried loot story, but it made for some interesting campfire tales.

The sun had dropped below the snowcapped peaks and the western horizon when we came up on the middle fork of the South Platte River. Not wanting to cross the river in the dark, we made camp on the northern side. The sky above was cloudless and cold as the temperature dropped when the sun took its dip to the west.

The stars were already out in all their grandeur as I got the fixings for a warming cook fire. Matt Lee took the chore of taking care of all the horses whilst I got us a supper fixing. Matt Lee had killed three large jackrabbits on the trail today to add to some fresh chicken eggs I had gotten in Fairplay for our supper. Timber, not to be outdone, had hunted down a jackrabbit for his own supper and had it sitting in his stomach long before our rabbits were done cooking on the spit over the fire.

Watching the man known as Ghost to his enemies as he ate, I could see the grief that surrounded him. Matt Lee's face showed the stress of living life now without a purpose. In our talks over a year ago on Kenosha Pass, he had flat out told me his whole reason for living life was to make sure Walk With Ghost was safe from harm. Not knowing what to say to the man for most of our supper, I said nothing at all. Finally, I asked that which I wondered about the most. "Matt Lee, once Connor is back with her Ma and Pa, do you plan on heading back to Redemption Valley?"

Matt Lee set his dinner plate down and stared at me for a spell as he pondered my question. Finally, he cleared his voice, "Take no offense Eric Robert, but even as I sit here with you enjoying this warm fire with a full stomach, I feel alone. I did not understand that grief and fear walked hand in hand; I grieve for my wife and at the same time I fear going on living without her. Losing her has shattered my life and has left me empty on the inside. If I was younger, there is no doubt that I would want to bounce back from this but Marshal, at my age now I am not so sure I have the wherewithal to do that. My only thought now is your granddaughter. It brings me more sorrow knowing they took her and that she may already be dead. This I cannot abide. I have promised you to see this through to the end even if it means my death. When you let Walk With Ghost and myself ride away from Kenosha Pass last year, you earned all that I can give. So for now I will focus in on that task of saving Connor from the Highlanders."

Ghost momentarily stopped speaking and stirred the ashes to the fire before adding two more logs. Then he began again, "Marshal, you deserve an answer to your question. As long as Walk With Ghost is buried in Redemption Valley, it will forever be my home. After this quest for Connor is complete and if I live, I have one other task I need to do, and that is to locate Walk With Ghost's son and tell him about his mother. Walk With Ghost's husband before me who had been a mountain man died in battle with the Arapahoe's when she was pregnant with his son. After Walk With Ghost became my wife, I gave her son my last name which he uses as his middle name, and he has only known me as his father. Our two natural sons both died in battle also fighting the Arapahoe's, but Dale Lee Patton survived the Arapahoe war. In some ways Dale was more like me than my own sons and he learned the way of the wilderness. Last I heard, he is over on the west slope of the Great Divide trapping in or near the Black Canyon close to Montrose. If I live through this, I believe I will find him and tell him of his mother's death."

Listening to Matt Lee, I felt his sorrow of what had happened and I believed him when he said he would lay down his life to rescue Connor. It was if the man called Ghost was more kin than those that had my blood running through their veins. We were both cut from the same cloth, and it would seem that we both had similar experiences and regrets in life. Clearing my voice, I said the only thing I was feeling, "Matt Lee, I am honored to have you ride by my side and if it is death that awaits us both, I could not think of anyone I would rather go out with than you."

Matt Lee chuckled and said, "Eric Robert, don't go getting teary eyed and calling us friends and such."

That made me laugh, and I replied, "Guess I should have added, 'If we don't go killing each other first.' Just for the record if you grab the pot to brew coffee - I will shoot you!"

With a chuckle Matt Lee said, "Understood!"

As the stars rained down their starlight, Timber faded into the high mountain grassland and the darkness. Maybe with all of Matt Lee's talk of loving his woman, he decided to try his luck tonight in finding his own lady love. I silently wished him the best in that regard. The wolf was here with us because he wanted to be here; I had no illusion that the wilderness called to him as it did to all the Lord's four-legged critters. It would not surprise me that Timber might just walk away one time and never come back.

After getting settled for the night and using my saddle as a pillow of sorts, I pondered about the trail ahead. Since I was a Federal Marshal, and this was my territory, I knew the way of the land well. It was roughly eighty miles to the mouth of the Phantom Canyon from where we were right now, and if the weather held only a three or four days' ride. I thought that the more easterly route by the ways of Lake George and Pikes Peak would be the easiest and quickest route and one I had ridden before.

Having decided on which trail to take, I thought some of what Matt Lee had said earlier. There is one thing that both of us knew in our hearts and even if we joked about it, we knew that no matter what we were better than friends now. We both would die for the other. It was the way it should be.

Chapter 7

Ghost and I both woke about the same time, which was an hour before dawn. The air was colder this morning, but the sky was still clear, and I could see the stars above as they faded from the night. Timber had rejoined us and was sleeping soundly to what was left of the fire.

Breakfast was a quick affair of leftover rabbit and unfrozen chicken eggs. Both Matt Lee and I took an hour this morning and cleaned and oiled our weapons. We even sharpened our Bowie knives on the whetstone. Both of us did not get to be the age we were without taking considerable care of our Winchesters, Colts, and Bowie knives. It was a ritual I enjoyed doing. It comforted me to know my weapons would be as ready as they could be for when I need them most.

As we were preparing our weapons, Timber once again faded into the mountain grass looking for his own breakfast. So far the wolf had been no bother at all on the trail.

Matt Lee also fed grain to Gypsy, Spirit, and Cimarron. Gypsy was feeling the grain as she tossed her head and pawed the earth with her hoof. She and the other horses were ready and willing for the trail ahead. They might not know where we were headed, but they were enthusiastic as long as there was an adventure in front of us.

By midday we approached the new town of Hartsel. Hartsel "The Heart of Colorado" was located just dead center of the state by my reckoning and had been founded by a rancher named Samuel Hartsel. More than once while riding through this country, I had stopped here and bathed in the hot springs just on the edge of town. There would be no time for such a luxury as that on this trip.

After Hartsel we headed almost due east and once again we crossed the middle fork of the South Platte as it meandered north to south through South Park. We stopped and refilled the canteens with some cool river water and ate some venison jerky.

Matt Lee was quiet on this day, and we spoke little other than what was needed to communicate on the trail.

The day as it wound down had gotten no warmer, and the night would be even colder. Just before sunset we set up camp and started a fire for the night. Once again Ghost saw to the horses, and I had the chore of fixing our feedbag for the night. Supper was my usual affair of fat back bacon, beans, and campfire tortillas. I brewed a pot of hot coffee and after taking a sip, I was mighty pleased with myself. After waiting until Ghost took a sip, I then asked, "How is the coffee, Matt Lee?"

Matt Lee, the aging mountain man, swirled some of my cowboy coffee around in his mouth and then he swallowed hard before speaking, "I have been shot, stabbed, left for dead, and even been run over by my own damn horse. I have endured privation, starvation, and suffered more hardships than most. Drinking this coffee has reminded me of those times."

Laughing out loud, I said, "It can't be all that bad."

Matt Lee now chuckled and started in again, "I have drunk rainwater from a mud puddle that tasted better than this; Guessing I should not have expected any better from a lawman with no campfire skills. Since my canteen is nearly empty, it will have to do in a pinch to wash down this meal you called supper."

With a smile plastered on my face, I asked "You want another cup?"

With smiling eyes, Matt Lee reached out his empty coffee cup and said, "I reckon I do, Eric Robert."

After refilling Matt Lee's coffee cup, I saw that Timber suddenly stood up and the hair on his back stood even taller. He was facing south into the night, and it was obvious from his reaction that something or someone was just beyond the campfire light. A full minute passed and then a man's voice from the direction that Timber was looking said, "Hello! Is that coffee I smell?"

I looked at Matt Lee who just shrugged his shoulder like a pesky fly had just landed on it. Not liking what I could not see, I replied, "It is, and you are welcome to a cup, but come easy, mister."

A man who was dressed as if he had seen better days stepped into the light, and Timber did not move one muscle as he was still looking to the south and past the man. Before I could say anything, Matt Lee said it first, "I don't take kindly to a man hiding in the shadows, so tell your compadres to show themselves and do it now or I will send the wolf out to fetch them."

As if on cue, Timber crouched and stepped forward one step as if waiting for the command. The man must not have seen Timber prior to his entrance into our camp, and now he almost looked as if he was ready to bolt. Running would not be a wise choice since Timber would only enjoy the chance to take the man down. I could see it in the eyes of the drifter that whatever he had in mind before coming into our camp, he was now regretting that decision. Still staring at Timber and unsure of himself, he said loudly, "Charley and Shoe, come on in and bring the horses; these gentlemen have been kind enough to offer us some coffee."

The drifter in front of me was dressed like a cowhand - a down on his luck cowhand. It seemed the only thing holding his clothes together was the dirt and grime that was abundant on his vest, shirt, and Levi jeans. His cattleman creased Stetson was almost just a rag of its former self and full of holes, and I wondered if it could even shade him from the sun let alone repel any rain. He wore a Colt in a tattered holster, and the pistol looked as if it had not been cleaned in ages. This man was trouble and anyone that rode with such a character would only be trouble as well. Speaking in a calm voice, "Tell Charley and Shoe to come easy."

Two men came in warily leading three horses that looked gaunt and hungry. Letting the reins of their horses loose, both men stepped cautiously closer. Charley and Shoe were dressed as shabbily as the first man. The first man with a fake smile spoke, "My name is Mark Maroon, and these are my partners Charley and Shoe."

When Mark introduced Charley and Shoe, he pointed out each when saying their names. Charley's eyes showed low intelligence and if I had to guess, he was just about as dimwitted as a man could be. The drifter named Shoe was a whole different breed altogether. His eyes showed high intelligence and if I was a betting man, Shoe was probably the most dangerous of the three. The metal on Shoe's Colt pistol gleamed as if it was just recently cleaned. And he wore it with the grip pointed forward on his right hip. In my experience men who wore their weapons in such a manner fancied themselves gunfighters. If this meeting went south, I would take out Shoe first. After studying the three drifters, I looked at Mark and spoke in a calm voice, "It looks as if the three of you are running from something or someone."

Mark's fake smile got even larger, and he spoke in a hurried voice, "Oh no, Mister! Not running from anyone; we have just had a run of bad luck. After finishing up a cattle drive down Texas way, we came to try our luck in the gold fields around Pikes Peak. As you can tell, we have had little luck in finding any of the elusive gold dust."

Matt Lee was still sitting down, but he had shifted his right leg slightly to make it easier to draw his weapon if the need called for it. Timber was as quiet as could be, but on alert and still half crouched in a threatening manner. Mark's and Charley's eyes kept glancing at Timber as they were trying to gauge how tamed the yellow-eyed wolf was. Matt Lee remained quiet and he let me do all the speaking. "We finished our supper and you are welcome to what is left of it and the coffee. Once you had your fill though, you will have to move on and be advised you will have to put a couple of miles in between us and you. We don't know you and do not cotton to try to sleep with strangers in the camp or even lurking nearby."

After we offered our remaining supper, Mark and Charley quickly got their own plates from their saddlebags and devoured the leftovers. Shoe kept staring at Ghost and moved more slowly than the other two as if he was pondering something that was bothering him. Once all three had finished what grub we had left, Mark looked to Timber and said, "I don't reckon I have ever seen a tamed wolf before with yellow eyes."

Ghost in a nonchalant way, "Make no mistake; he is not tamed, and he is no wolf. He is the devil wearing a white fur coat. And if you feel the need to pet him, that four-legged devil will chew off your hand!"

That shut Mark up and you could see in his and Charley's eyes that they wanted to be anywhere but here at this moment. Shoe seemed not to be as taken in by Ghost's words and while staring at the aging mountain man he said, "I finally figured it out. I saw you once in Como and I know who you are, but I thought someone had killed you about a year ago. You are that mountain man Matt Lee that fought all those Ute Indians years ago in some sort of one man war."

What I had feared the most when I asked Matt Lee to come along in the attempt to get my granddaughter back was someone recognizing him. There still was that $2000 bounty hanging out there waiting to be claimed. Shoe was still staring at Ghost when Matt Lee spoke, "That man you speak of died on Kenosha Pass about a year ago. And if you want to think differently, it might just be the worst thought you have ever had, son."

Mark and Charley had all but forgotten Timber and me, and they were now staring at Ghost. His name and reputation were something no man could ever forget. Shoe stood slowly as he spoke again, "Mark and Charley, if I recollect correctly, there is a $2000 dead or alive bounty on Matt Lee for killing some soldiers in Grand Lake!"

Now everyone stood slowly including myself as this encounter was now heading south. Ghost spoke in a voice as if he was just having a low-keyed conversation over dinner, "Son, before you get any foolish thoughts about collecting a bounty, I have to ask you what do you see when you look at me or my friends?"

Shoe smiled when asked that question and he replied, "What I see is a raggedy dog and two old men way past their prime, and I wonder if they could even put on their breeches this morning without tipping over."

Chapter 8

Ghost still in his easygoing manner, "The likes of men like you should be more cautious of old men that still wander the timberline that has claimed the lives of much younger men."

The drifter named Shoe stood his ground, and the tension was thick enough to cut with a knife, and I knew Matt Lee's mind had already switched to his killer instinct. I almost felt sorry for the three down-and-out drifters as their eyes showed desperation, and I knew the temptation of the $2000 bounty was more than they could walk away from. Trying to stop the death of the three men, I said, "Shoe, nobody is dead yet and you can still walk away!"

Shoe said in a voice that sounded like a plea, "We have no money, food, home, or anybody to walk away to!"

Shoe drew his weapon first, followed by Charley and Mark - none of whom had the skill or the speed of Ghost or myself. Ghost drew and fired his Colt twice before Shoe cleared leather. His first bullet caught Shoe at the center point of his chest just where his ribs came together. His second bullet cut a path in the front and out of the back of his throat. Mark was no luckier as I shot him through the brain pan just above his nose. Charley the dimwit was taken down by Timber and before Shoe's or Mark's bodies hit the ground, Timber had already ripped the young man's throat out in the savage attack. Shoe and Mark were both dead when they dropped, but Charley was not so lucky. With both hands trying to stop the flow of blood from his ravaged throat, it took almost a full minute before he bled out and the life withered from his eyes.

Life was harsh here in the Rocky Mountain frontier and death was swift. Death and violence were not something new to Ghost or myself, but it still bothered me; it could have so easily been avoided. The drifters should have just drifted. Ghost and I quickly reloaded our spent shells out of habit, and Timber, awash with Charley's blood, sat down calmly and licked his white fur cleaning himself.

The night was still young, and Ghost and I scratched out one shallow grave for the three wannabe bounty hunters and rolled their bodies in. Ghost listened with his hat in his hand as I said the Lord's Prayer over those whom I believe if the situation had been reversed would not have given us the respect or courtesy of a Christian burial.

After burying the three wannabe bandits, we unsaddled the drifters' horses and took off their reins and halters and released them. Hopefully, someone who could care for them properly would claim them for their own. We laid the saddles on top of the graves for anyone who happened by that might need them.

By the time we were finished with burying the bodies of the drifters and letting their horses loose, the moon was directly overhead as we rolled out our bedrolls. The silence of the night crept in and even the normal night sounds stayed quiet as if the woods that surrounded us knew death had overtaken our camp.

The air beyond the warmth of the fire was frosting the aspens and evergreens. The aspen leaves of autumn were becoming less and less as the closing winter made them fall from the tree limbs that had given them life. The circle of life and death was constant and the out of luck drifters' lives had come full circle here this evening. Taking their lives was something I would have wished to avoid, but they left us no choice. It had been them or us.

Just as I had finally pushed the death faces of Mark, Charley, and Shoe to the back of my mind, Ghost spoke, "The man named Shoe was right about one thing."

Rolling over to face Ghost as he lay four feet away, I asked with curiosity in my voice, "And what would that be, Matt Lee?"

Ghost remained quiet for a few seconds and then replied, "I can't put on my breeches without tipping over."

Even with the smell of death still hanging in the air, I laughed and laughed hard at what Ghost had said. Still laughing, I said, "Same here old man, same here."

The morning came faster than I would have wanted since we had only gotten about four hours of shuteye. Both Ghost and I woke just before dawn and set into doing our morning chores. Ghost readied the horses as I took on the campfire duties of making an edible breakfast.

Once I was planted in my saddle on Gypsy, I looked one last time at the graves of those that had died the night before. I felt no remorse for Mark, Charley, and Shoe for they had brought the thunder down on themselves, but it reminded me of how quickly death came to those who have lost hope.

Timber had rejoined us after some time in the woods, which I assumed he used in hunting down and then eating his own breakfast. The wolf's white fur was snowy white again after being painted red with the blood of the dimwitted Charley. It would seem that the yellow-eyed dog took care in his appearance. Chuckling to myself, I thought, "Hell, it would seem Timber was more of a dandy than Ghost or myself."

By noon we stopped for a few minutes and refreshed our canteens and let the horses get their fill from a small brook south of the railroad tracks. The tracks I believed were a subsidiary of the Atchison, Topeka and Santa Fe Railway called the Colorado Midland Railroad. The railroad business was something I knew nothing about, and it seemed that the railroads that served the Rocky Mountain frontier and the gold and silver mines were always going broke and changing ownership. For an aging lawman, the railroads and their ownership were always confusing. To be rich and own a railroad is not a life I would envy.

Just before sunset we had reached an area some had called Lake George. I had to laugh at that name because Lake George was just a hollow in the ground that some man named George had dammed in and when the snowmelt that flowed into his makeshift dam froze, he would then cut the ice into blocks to be hauled by the railroads to Colorado Springs in the east. It would seem that some made gold out of ice. I had yet to decipher if George was not playing with a full deck or if he was a business genius.

Ghost had shot three rabbits for our supper this evening as I readied the campfire. Fresh meat was always welcome, and it would seem Ghost and Timber had a knack for hunting while riding the trail to our destination. That night after supper, under the cold night sky and the stars, I pondered what lay ahead in Phantom Canyon.

Phantom Canyon was almost due south of our position by my reckoning forty-two or forty-three miles. At least another three days riding depending if old man winter stepped aside for our travel. We had left the high mountain grasslands of South Park and now we would travel the woods and timber that meandered through the mountains. I had no plan on what to do when we finally meet up with the Scottish outlaws. We would have to survey the situation and make a plan of attack on the move. My priority first was to get my granddaughter to safety even if that meant leaving the Scottish bandit Alistair McPherson and his brother Alban alive.

Taking out the tintype of Connor, I looked at her likeness again and was stunned at how much she looked like her mother and grandmother. I hoped and prayed that Connor had the strength and insight of my daughter and former wife. What had happened to her would scar her physically and mentally if she did not. My gut instinct told me differently; I knew she had my blood running through her veins, and she would be tougher than most girls her age. Still staring at the tintype, I smiled and my heart sang with love for my granddaughter even though I had never met the young girl. I wondered how that could be; then I dismissed that thought as quickly as it was born, and I knew it was just predestined to be.

Tucking the tintype back into my vest pocket, I realized that Ghost had been watching me the whole time I was looking at the tintype of Connor. Not wanting to seem weak in front of a man such as Matt Lee I said, "Just looking at her likeness again so I will remember what Connor looks like when the time is right."

Ghost smiled and his eyes showed compassion when he spoke, "Well, Marshal, we both know that is bullshit. Even with all the death that has surrounded me in my life, I know love when I see it.

I reckon I looked just as you did looking at Connor's likeness every morning when I woke up with Walk With Ghost by my side. The love for that little girl you have never met is genuine and the way it is supposed to be, my friend. Just know Eric Robert, for you and Connor I will move heaven and earth to bring her home and if needed - I will kill every son of a bitch that made her or yours suffer!"

Looking at the man who not so long ago was my foe, but never my enemy I replied, "Ghost, your friendship is something I will always treasure. Afterwards, when this is said and done and when Connor is older, I will bring her to visit you in your hidden valley."

Ghost was quiet for a long spell and he faced skyward and gazed upon the starlight, and he said in a voice I think was meant more for himself than for me, "The night before you entered my valley, I had a vision and a dream. The spirit of my grandfather who died when I was young spoke to me and told me of your coming and your quest to free your granddaughter. From this vision, there were two things I learned, Eric Robert. The first was we would secure Connor's release. The second thing was I would never return to Redemption Valley!"

Chapter 9

For the next two days as we traveled to the mouth of Phantom Canyon, Ghost became almost silent and spoke only when it was necessary along the trail. During this time he neither joked nor bitched about my coffee, so I knew his mind was busy with other things. His thinker seemed to be in deep thought, and I wondered if it was the killing of the drifters or that he had revealed his vision to me of his grandfather stating he would never return to Redemption Valley that brought the silence. It could be as simple as it was his way of dealing with the grief of losing Walk With Ghost. Matt Lee, a man who had led a simple life, was a complicated man in so many ways. I saw no reason to engage him in conversation if he had the mind not to talk. I would leave him to his own thoughts for now.

Even though Matt Lee claimed to have no hold on the white wolf with yellow eyes, Timber seemed loyal to the bone to the aging mountain man. When the trail was wide enough, Timber matched the stride walking side by side of Ghost and Cimarron. When the trail narrowed, Timber followed behind Matt Lee as if he was given an unspoken command. At night after Timber had foraged his own meal, he would not sleep with Matt Lee but within an arm's length of the man. On the nights I was sleepless thinking about what lay ahead, I would find Timber looking toward Matt Lee. It would seem that the white wolf with yellow eyes knew Ghost was a troubled man, and he was overseeing and protecting the man in the only way he knew how. These days on the trail I had come to realize that the white wolf loved the aging mountain man as much as Matt Lee loved Timber. I chuckled to myself that it would seem that both Ghost and Timber just tolerated me - and I was okay with that.

Although it had been cold, the weather held since the shoot-out with the wannabe bounty hunters Mark, Charley, and Shoe. The skies had remained cloudless as we entered the recently new mining settlement of Cripple Creek, Colorado. The settlement was formed when Robert Miller "Bob" Womack discovered gold near here. Shortly after Womack's first discovery W.S. Stratton located the largest gold vein in recent history and started the Independence Mine.

Stratton was the one from whom the Highlanders had kidnapped his granddaughter and after paying the $100,000 ransom, they still sold her down south to the Mexican bandits. It would seem the Scottish bandit Alistair McPherson and his brother Alban and their band of brigands had nothing to fear from the local law. The Highlanders may have had nothing to fear from the local law, but a grandfather's wrath was a whole different matter. The priority, if my granddaughter Connor was still alive, was getting her home safe to her mother and father. If she was already sold to the Mexicans, then getting her back from them would take precedence. If she was dead, then there was nothing I would not do in wreaking vengeance on those that had a party in her death.

We were short on supplies and needed grain for the horses so we stopped at a dry good store on what served as the Main Street in Cripple Creek. Timber, as was becoming the routine, appealed to every young boy's and girl's imagination and attention as they followed us as we made our way through the settlement. It would seem traveling without being noticed as I had wanted to do was nothing more than a fantasy. The road in front of Stratton Dry Goods had seen better days. The dirt road was rutted by wagons to the point it was almost impassable by anything other than a horse or a man on foot. After tying Gypsy, Cimarron, and Spirit to the hitching rail Ghost, Timber, and I walked into the dry goods store. Once we had our provisions packed away on the horses, we made ready our weapons. Once that task was completed, Ghost and I walked across the street to the Imperial Hotel & Saloon.

In the ransom note delivered in Alma to my daughter Jessica and her husband Brody which I now had in my vest pocket, someone detailed it that whoever brought the $100,000 was to make first contact at the Imperial Saloon in Cripple Creek. Also, both of us had a hankering for a beef steak fried up by someone else. If we were lucky, maybe they had some fruit pie to satisfy our sweet tooth.

The saloon was the typical fair of an upstart mining town. It had bat-wing doors as most saloons, but it also had a second set of full doors that were wide open behind the bat-wings that were used when the cold high mountain air became unbearable. Before entering, Ghost and I palmed our Colt pistols just to make sure they were not hung up in our holsters because of the dampness of the air. Knowing our weapons were free and easy, we slid them back into our holsters. Using the tip of my Winchester, I opened the right side of the bat-wing door and we stepped slowly in.

The room was not large and there were a half-dozen tables with four to six chairs at each table. There was a potbelly stove almost in the center roaring red hot heating the room to a comfortable level. The saloon was busy with twenty-five or so miners and ranch hands since it was feeding time at high noon. The hardwood bar with its shiny brass footrest and spit-shined spittoons was full with patrons. There was one empty table however that was the farthest back in the room and faced the door which was to our liking and we headed for it. Timber followed us and seemed curious of the miners, cowboys, and the saloon.

Ghost and I took up both seats that put our backs to the wall so we could survey the room. No one took notice of us or even Timber. I believe no one had even glanced our way once we had entered. Everyone was focused on what they were doing. I asked Ghost, "How do you want to play it, Matt Lee?"

Ghost gave the saloon another look over before he spoke, "However you want, Marshal. I will follow your lead until you need me to jump in."

Nodding my head "yes," I added, "I say we order first and then we will ask around for the associates of the McPhersons."

A bald-headed man with a bushy handlebar mustache and a dirty apron took our order of rare beef steaks, taters, a shot of whiskey, and a cup of coffee for each of us. Once that was done, and I knew the food would be on its way, I stood and drew my Colt and with my arm bent at the elbow and the pistol pointed skywards, I had second thoughts. Looking at Matt Lee I said, "I did not take notice if there was a second floor above us. I would hate to put a hole in some soiled dove while she was working."

Matt Lee looked at me and sort of rolled his eyes before he spoke, "Might be rooms out back where they ply their trade. There are no rooms above us. I reckon you are safe to blow a hole in the ceiling if that is what you have in mind."

Before I fired my attention getter, the bald-headed man showed up with our steaks and was a bit leery setting them on the table in front of us since I was standing with my pistol pointed up toward the heavens. The man with the dirty apron backed away slowly, still looking at me. Once he was a safe distance, I fired my pistol.

The sound of my shot was intensified in close quarters, and the smell of burnt gunpowder filled the air. After more than a few "Holy shits and what the hells," the room became quiet and every miner and cowpoke was now looking in our direction. Ghost was still seated and calmly cut into his steak. I let the first initial shock of firing my pistol wear off before I said in a matter-of-fact voice, "We have ridden a great distance to meet any acquaintances of the McPhersons. We have something they want and they have something we want. We were told the Imperial Saloon was the place to ask about their whereabouts. So I am asking. Are any of those Scottish assholes in here?"

I was not sure if it was the firing of my pistol or calling the McPhersons assholes, but it had the same effect as starting the saloon on fire. Everyone decided to skedaddle out of there in a rush leaving only the bald headed man with the handlebar mustache that worked the Imperial Saloon and two other gents. Both stood slowly, but both looked too stupid to be the bosses and it was highly unlikely that I was looking at the Alistair McPherson and his brother Alban also known as the Highlanders. Both remaining men were dressed as cowboys wearing Levi jeans and flannel shirts. The cowboy hats by the looks of them were cattleman crease and had the look of being made by Stetson. Each had a tied down well-cared for Colt still in their holsters with the grips pointed backwards for a standard draw. The taller one with blonde hair spoke first. "I would not go around shooting off your pistol and calling the bosses assholes if I were you!"

Out of the corner of my eye, I could see Ghost still eating his steak as if nothing had happened, but he had a smile from ear to ear. He was enjoying his steak and this encounter. After I fired off my pistol, Timber sat up and his ears perked straight up in the air and seemed to take it all in. I rolled around what the tall outlaw had said before replying, "I reckon we can compromise!"

That confused the tall one, and he frowned some when he asked, "Compromise?"

In a calm voice I said, "Yes, compromise. How about you live your life and I live mine!"

His face clouded over with anger, and he wanted to draw, but he wasn't as dumb as he looked and held the urge. He didn't like me and I sure as hell didn't like him. His anger faded almost as quickly as it had appeared and after a full minute of pondering what to do, the blonde-headed outlaw finally said, "Look, we have business to discuss, and we can settle this later if you have a mind to. For now the boss has instructions for you. Can we join you?"

Knowing full well that these two posed no threat for now unless they had the money in hand so I quickly responded, "Yep, you can join us, but don't expect any free drinks!"

Out of the corner of my eye, I caught Ghost's smile and eye roll again as he was still eating his steak and taters. Both outlaws looked at each other and if I could read their minds, they were both pondering, "What the hell is up with this guy?"

Both outlaws walked cautiously across the room and as I holstered my Colt, I looked toward the bald-headed man who was now leaning on the bar watching our encounter with a smile. Waiting until both outlaws were almost to my table, I said to the barman, "I hope you caught that sir; neither my friend nor I will buy any drinks for these two."

Both outlaws out of instinct turned to the barman as the barkeep chuckled and replied, "Got it, no free drinks for the likes of those two."

Chapter 10

The two outlaws from the Highlanders gang were a tad confused when they finally settled into the seats at our table directly across from Ghost and myself, and both looked as if they had just sat down into a fresh cow pie. The tall, blonde one was directly across from me, and the short dark-haired one was directly across from Matt Lee.

Out of the corner of my eye, I saw Matt Lee silently pull his Colt as the kidnappers slowly took their seats. The Ghost's weapon was hidden under the table, and neither of the outlaws had seen the movement. Feeling loose and hungry, I started to eat my steak and taters.

Everything I had done since firing off my pistol into the ceiling was aimed at changing the pecking order. The kidnappers wanted to believe they were calling the shots and ramrodding this meeting. I thought it was essential to keep them muddled and to put Ghost and myself in charge of this get-together. The lap dogs for Alistair McPherson and his brother Alban and in time the rest of the

Highlanders gang themselves needed to know we were not to be trifled with. What these men of the Highlander gang did not know was there was no gold or cash to pay the ransom and that we intended on taking my granddaughter Connor back by force.

At first the tall, blonde-headed bandit seemed out of sorts when he first sat down as he watched me eat my steak and taters as if they were not there at all. A full minute passed and with both elbows on the table, I finally looked up from my meal and acted as if I had just seen them sitting there in front of me. After swallowing a piece of steak, I pointed my fork at the plate of food and said in casual conversation, "This is superb steak and it is very tender. I always liked a good tender steak. If you boys are hungry, you should order one. Remember, you have to pay for it yourself; my associate and I do not buy drinks or steaks for assholes."

The anger flared up again in the eyes of the one sitting directly across from me, and he slammed his palms down on the table so hard it would have overturned my coffee cup if I hadn't caught it just in time. The blonde-headed outlaw took several seconds to calm himself before he spoke in an irritated tone, "That is enough! I will not tolerate your talking to me like that! I am surprised that a rich mine owner would send two over-the-hill old farts to pay the ransom for his granddaughter. You need to listen and listen closely. I will only tell you the boss's instructions once and you better heed what I got to say. Do I make myself clear?"

Looking directly into the blonde-headed kidnapper's eyes, I said as calmly as if he had asked if I had wanted more coffee, "I hear you because your voice sort of carries and you seem a tad bit angry. So spill the beans. What does your boss want us to do?"

Still angry and trying to control his voice, the tall kid-snatcher said, "First things first. I am supposed to verify that you have the $100,000. You need to take us to where it is hidden so we can see it."

Cutting off another piece of steak, I acted as if I was pondering his request. After swallowing another piece of tender steak, I said, "I don't think so."

That shut him up for a full minute, and the tall bandit was at a loss for words until he replied, "I don't think so?"

Pointing my fork at him with a piece of steak dangling from it, I said in a casual tone, "Yes, that is correct. Where I come from, 'I don't think so' means NO! I do not believe I can be any clearer than that."

The bandit and lap dog for his Scottish boss slammed his palms down so hard this time it did knock over both of our coffee cups and in an angry retort, "MISTER, I DON'T THINK YOU KNOW WHO YOU ARE DEALING WITH!"

This time I never took my eyes off of the desperado in front of me and said in a tone to match my seriousness, "The problem here is that neither you nor your boss understand who you are dealing with. So let me show you. MATT!"

Matt Lee jumped in just as he said he would and promptly shot the dark-haired bandit sitting across from him through the table. The wood of the table slowed the bullet some, so there was no exit wound as the short dark-haired outlaw tipped over backwards and hit the floor hard. He shuddered twice from the wound just below his upper ribcage just before he died.

The blonde-haired outlaw was so startled at what had just transpired that he was momentarily in shock and all he could do was look at his dead compadre lying on the floor. After shooting the kidnapper, Ghost quickly stood up and now leveled his Colt at the taller bandit's head.

Timber stood just as quickly as Ghost, and the wolf sauntered around the table and sniffed the still warm corpse of the dark-haired outlaw. Timber, doing what his kind did, marked his territory by lifting his leg and peeing on the man's forehead. It all seemed sort of fitting.

The tall blonde-headed outlaw now knew who was in charge. All his anger faded quickly as he looked first at the killing end of Matt Lee's pistol and then at me. In a high-pitched voice the outlaw asked, "What the hell did he do that for?"

A smile spread across my face when I answered his question. "My associate is a tad slow and I think it just dawned on him you called him an over-the-hill old fart. I reckon he didn't cotton much to that remark."

Sweat had beaded on the remaining outlaw's head as he wondered if his death was near. He finally asked another question in an almost silent tone, "Who are you guys?"

I did not want the Highlanders man to know I had a personal stake in all of this. If they knew Connor was my granddaughter, they could use it as leverage against me. I let him sweat for another full minute before I answered him, "We are just a couple of gents hired to bring the young girl home safe. We can do it with no more bloodshed or kill all of you. My associate and I couldn't care less how it turns out. The O'Brien's will pay us the same either way."

The outlaw now was broken just like a wild mustang. He had no reply and sat silently across from me. Seeing this, I took him by the reins and led him where I wanted him to go. "Now we have gotten all that settled, tell me where we can exchange the $100,000 for the young girl."

The now subdued outlaw looked as if he was about ready to bust a tear or two. He cleared his voice not trusting it not to come out as a whimper, "Head southeast five miles to the mining camp of Victor and then two more miles to the mouth of Phantom Canyon. The canyon runs north and south and at the mouth of the canyon is a large white boulder standing all by its lonesome on the west side of the trail. Start a campfire and soon after the exchange will happen there."

Ghost put his Colt back in his holster and then sat down and looked toward the barkeep who looked as he was in shock of what had just happened almost as much as the outlaw. Ghost, in a matter-of-fact tone asked, "Sir, do you have any fruit pie?"

The bald-headed man cleared his face and in an almost stutter, "Why yes sir, we have apple pie for two bits a slice."

Ghost looked at me and I nodded my head "yes." Then he looked at the still breathing outlaw and then glanced back to the man with the handlebar mustache and said, "Bring us two slices of apple pie. Wait, make that three slices and an extra fork."

Our table was silent for the next three minutes or so as the bartender rustled up the apple pie and then brought us three plates and one more fork. Approaching the table cautiously, the bald-headed barkeep set a slice of pie in front of both Ghost and myself. He then stood there momentarily not knowing what to do with the third slice and fork. I pointed at the table in front of the tall outlaw, and the barkeep set the final piece of the pie and the fork in front of the blonde-headed outlaw. Before the barkeep could turn to leave, I reached in my vest pocket and produced a twenty dollar gold piece and handed it to the barkeep and said, "Will this cover the cost of the meal and repair of the hole in the ceiling and for the cleanup of that asshole on the floor?"

The handlebar mustached barkeep's face lit up with a smile and quickly replied, "Why yes sir, more than enough and I thank you."

After the barkeep had moved back to the bar, I took my fork and wedged off a piece of pie and placed it in my mouth, savoring the apple, cinnamon, sugar and the crisp crust and remarking, "This is some mighty fine pie."

Ghost nodded his head in agreement since he had already finished his slice of pie. Pointing to the untouched pie in front of the bandit, I said, "Better finish up your pie mister before my associate gets an inkling you don't like his hospitality and takes a disliking to you."

The blonde-headed brigand looked at me and then Ghost in total disbelief and was about to say something but then changed his mind and picked up the fork in front of him and quickly ate his pie.

The bandit finished his pie before I did. Once I set my fork down after finishing my pie, I looked him in the eye and said, "Tell your boss and his brother we will head to Phantom Canyon come first light and the young girl better be there and if one hair on her head is out of place, he will have to answer for that."

The tall outlaw still subdued with all that had happened answered quickly, "Yes sir!"

Holding the man with only my eyes, I let a full minute pass before saying, "You may leave now."

The outlaw stood slowly and once gaining his feet, he turned and with shaking knees started for the bat-wing doors. Before he could exit, I said in his direction, "Wait a minute."

The bandit turned slowly in my direction and the sweat started on his brow once again. There was fear in his eyes, and I could tell he was now expecting to end up just like his friend, lying dead on the floor. I pointed toward the bald-headed barkeep standing behind the bar and said, "You owe the man two bits for the pie."

Chapter 11

The tall blonde-headed outlaw looked as dazed as if a horse had kicked him in the head. He looked at me with almost vacant eyes and slowly walked back to the barkeep and laid two bits on the bar in front of him. After paying for the pie, he walked slowly as if the pie had already made a quick exit and had filled his trousers. He walked out through the bat-wing doors without looking at Ghost or myself. On his way out he passed a man wearing a gold star that had the word sheriff stamped on it.

Cripple Creek's sheriff was a man I knew and his name was Con Adams. Con Adams was not a man that could be trusted; it was he that let the Highlander gang roam this area with no interference from the local law. If truth be known and I was a betting man, he was being paid to look the other way by Connor's kidnappers. Con was a dangerous man in his own right and had been in several gunfights where he had come out the victor. He was younger than myself by at least twenty years and had short, dark hair with a clean-shaven face. He dressed fancy for a mining settlement with dark trousers and a white button-down shirt with a black vest. His gun rig was a shiny black leather holster with a well-cared for 44 Colt resting in its sheath with the grip pointed backwards for a standard draw.

Con walked over and stood above the dead man on the floor and then pointed to him while looking at me and saying, "Eric, do you know who that man is?"

Without standing I said in a matter-of-fact voice, "No I do not. The one thing I know Con, is that he will never be the same fellow he was before."

Sheriff Adams stood for a spell just looking at me trying to decipher what I was doing here and why he now had a dead body of one of the Highlander gang lying on the floor of the Imperial Saloon. Looking at the barkeep and pointing to the dead outlaw, he said, "Randall, will you please remove this man. It is bad for my sheriff business and your saloon business if we leave bodies lying around."

The barkeep was quick to move and said, "Yes Sheriff, I can drag him into the back room until I can get some of the boys to help get him down to the undertaker."

Silence was stifling in the room as Randall dragged the man that Ghost had killed into the back room. Once the barkeep and the dead man were now out of sight, Con pointed at the chair in front of me and said in a slightly annoyed voice, "May I?"

Timber, the whole time that Con had been in the room and during the removal of the dead outlaw, had been lying down in between Ghost and my chair. He seemed to sleep as if this was just another normal day in the yellow-eyed wolf's life.

I nodded my head "yes" and then Con took a seat, and he looked at Ghost for a few moments before returning his gaze to me before speaking, "As sheriff of this settlement, I have a few questions and one observation. Let's start with the questions. "Why are you here in Cripple Creek, Marshal? Why is the famous Eric Robert not wearing a badge? What is up with the white wolf?"

Trying to keep my name and the fact I was a federal Marshal out of this now was not possible since it now involved Con Adams. Even though I did not like the man, he was the sheriff here and the questions he asked were legit and needed to be answered. So instead of beating around the bush I told it to him straight. "Alistair

McPherson and his brother Alban kidnapped my granddaughter Connor and are holding her for a $100,000 ransom. I have come here to negotiate her release. The reason I am not wearing a badge is I am here as a grandfather looking out for the welfare of my kin and it may turn bloody. You already know - with what has already happened and what will happen in the next couple of days - that it may straddle the fence of what is lawful and what is not, hence why I am not sporting a badge to your fair burg. As for the white wolf, he is his own man and can leave at any time. I reckon he has become accustomed to us and seems to want to stay. I would also suggest that if you want to keep your hand, I would not try to pet him; he does not cotton to strangers. Now you asked your questions, so what is your observation, Sheriff Adams?"

Con Adams rolled the answers to his questions around some as he looked at me before he answered. "Given the circumstances of why you and your companions are here, I feel that what happened here in the Imperial Saloon today was justifiable and not in need of further investigation on my part."

Con now took his eyes off of me and they now landed on Ghost. "My observation Eric Robert, is that it would seem that the famous mountain man Matt Lee also known as Ghost is still alive and well. It would seem that the rumors of the legend's passing were just that...rumors."

The tension at our table was almost unbearable as we all now sat in silence. After a full two minutes with nothing more to add, Con Adams put both of his hands on top of the table to push off to stand. I quickly grabbed both by the wrist and with all my strength I pinned them to the top of the table. As Con tried in vain to wrestle his hands free from my death grip, I said what needed to be added to the conversation. Speaking in an attention-getting voice, "I need to be clear on something Con. Alistair McPherson and his brother Alban do not know I am the kidnapped girl's grandpa and this tidbit of information they cannot know. If Matt Lee or I survive this encounter and we think just for a second you gave that information to the Highlanders, that badge and your Colt cannot stop one of us from killing you. You need to ponder that for a spell before you go talking to the McPhersons. It does not take a long stretch of the imagination that the Highlanders operate freely in your jurisdiction without your getting a cut of their ill-gotten gains.

Now I am going to release your hands and if you feel the need to pull that pistol, then you need to pull it and hope for the best."

If anger that had flooded the Cripple Creek's sheriff's eyes as I pinned his hands to the table could strike a man dead, then I would be dead. The initial flush of anger left Con's eyes just to be replaced by hatred, but reasoning. He knows he could not survive a shoot-out with both Ghost and myself. Con Adams may be a corrupt sheriff, but my thought was he was not a stupid man. Con might feel that his honor or reputation had just been disrespected and draw anyway. Either or, I released his wrists slowly. Con stood straight up and his face was still red from wrath, and his eyes never left mine. He stood still, and I thought he would draw, which would be a huge mistake on his part. After running it through his mind of his chances in besting both Ghost and myself and recognizing that the odds were not in his favor, he turned and walked out the bat-wing doors without saying another word.

After Con Adams had made his exit, Ghost said, "I reckon the sheriff was used to more of a cordial hello from a fellow peace officer than just what had happened. Do you think he will tell the Highlanders who we really are?"

Looking toward the barkeep that had overheard the conversation that had just taken place between Con Adams and myself, I said to Ghost but looking towards Randall, "Not so sure what Con will do. I reckon he will do whatever he thinks gains him the advantage. If he ponders out that keeping quiet is the best benefit of his situation here, then he will keep quiet. Not so sure about Randall over there. What do you think is your best benefit, Randall?"

Randall was all ears as he stood straight up and pointed at his own chest. He spoke with a hurried voice, "Who me? I reckon mister that if any part of that conversation was meant for me, I would have been paying closer attention. I want to make it known to both of you gentlemen that I do not agree with the sheriff on what he or the McPhersons do. Matter of fact, if they were not around Cripple Creek, it would be a right nice place to live."

Reaching into my vest pocket, I produced another twenty dollar gold piece and tossed it across the saloon. Randall proved to be a skilled man in the ways of catching money and snatched it out of the air as I replied to him, "You need to keep quiet about us for a couple of days Randall until we get what we came for"

Randall's face now was a smile from ear to ear as he pocketed the gold piece and said, "Understood Sir!"

Chapter 12

Ghost, after seeing me pay another twenty dollar gold piece to the barkeep, chuckled and said, "Are you sure you don't have that $100,000 in your vest pocket? If I didn't know better, I would say you are showing off for the ladies with all that gold...except there aren't any ladies in here to show off to."

Chuckling myself, I replied, "Just paying for the cleanup of the mess you left on the floor here Matt Lee, as a good compadre would. My thought is that we have made an impression today and we should probably take our leave. I believe we should take the horses to that livery stable we passed on the way into Cripple Creek and hold up there for the night with the horses. I would feel better having Timber, Gypsy, Spirit, and Cimarron close for their ears and eyes while we catch some shut eye and in case we need to hightail it out of here in a hurry."

Ghost nodded his head in agreement as he said, "Sounds like a plan Eric Robert, since it would seem we might have overstayed our welcome in Sheriff Con Adams' town."

After paying a smidgen extra to stay with the horses through the night, I slept underneath Gypsy, and Ghost slept in the same stall as Cimarron. Spirit had her own stall all for herself. Timber slept outside the stalls in the runway in between the front and rear stable's doors. I believe the white wolf was doing his best to ensure Matt Lee's and my safety as he could only do.

The stable had a roof and was enclosed except for the entrance, and I was thankful for that since the wind had picked up and was howling and rocking the rough-hewed structure. The wind and the cold did not keep me awake, but trying to plan out the day tomorrow when we would take Connor back from the McPhersons did keep my mind pondering. However, I rolled it around in my brain pan, and I could not come up with a good plan on how to take my granddaughter back safely. I finally decided I would have to do it like most events in my life happened and that was to let fate and destiny take over. Having decided there was no plan and that all the worrying would not change that, I fell asleep.

Gypsy nudged me awake with the tip of her nose. Looking up into her big brown eyes, I had a feeling of guilt flood over me. In all that had happened in recent days, I had not given her the love she was accustomed to getting from me. After standing and dusting off the straw from the stall, I pulled Gypsy in close and hugged her neck tightly hoping she would forgive me. She folded the best a full-grown horse could into my arms as if she was telling me it was okay to be distracted and that she was on my side. I loved this horse more than life itself; she had been closer than any friend or companion in my life up until now. Gypsy girl deserved better than me, but I was all she had.

Opening the stall door to give me more room to saddle Gypsy, I saw Timber for the first time this morning and the yellow-eyed, white wolf was just finishing his breakfast. It would seem that someone in Cripple Creek would be shy one cat. It would seem that you can take Timber the wolf out of the wilderness and into a town, but you cannot take the wilderness out of the wolf. It would seem the laws of nature were just the same here in town as they were along the Rocky Mountain frontier. Those that are weaker always became prey for those that are stronger. Hell, I would not lose much sleep over it since every cat I ever met was a selfish critter that bossed its owner around. Timber stopped chomping on his kitty meal and looked at me with curiosity. I pointed at what was left of the cat and said, "Bon appetite my furry friend."

After getting all the horses saddled and packed for the trail to Phantom Canyon, Matt Lee turned and asked, "Do you think it would be wise to go to the Imperial Saloon for some breakfast?"

Letting Ghost's question soak in for a few seconds, I looked at Timber as he was licking his paws cleaning himself from his breakfast and I replied, "I couldn't care less if it is wise or not; if I don't get some chow, I will be hunting cats for my breakfast."

Ghost chuckled as he pulled his pistol to check his loads and then said, "If that steak and pie last night was any sign of how good their breakfast is, I would fight my way past a passel of folks for some bacon and chicken eggs."

Checking my loads in my Colt as well, I said, "Well said my friend. Let's go get some bacon and eggs."

Breakfast was uneventful and the chicken eggs and bacon were fantastic. Not knowing the next time we would have such grub at a sit down table, Ghost and I finished with a slice of pie. The saloon was packed with men with their feed bags on, but it was absent of Con Adams and any of the Highlanders gang. No one seemed to take particular notice of Ghost, Timber, or myself.

After the meal and once back in the saddle, I pointed Gypsy southeast into the rising sun. The skies were lit with a magnificent Colorado orange and blue sunrise as the day just like every other day started. It made me grateful to be alive and able to ride the high country. The wind was chilled and was pushing slightly to the back of our winter dusters. Turning my collar up and pulling my hat a tad lower helped some in keeping the breeze at bay as we pushed on toward Phantom Canyon. After giving Gypsy a slight jab of my spur I said to Ghost, "Let's go get my granddaughter."

Ghost followed suit with Cimarron as he led Spirit and replied, "I reckon so, Marshal Robert."

We passed the sheriff's office as we left Cripple Creek and Con Adams was standing on the boardwalk leaning against a flagpole that flew the flags of Colorado and the United States. He gave me the ole' stink eye as I rode past him. It was yet to be seen if he had informed the Scottish bandits Alistair McPherson or his brother Alban of my true relationship with Connor. It bothered me some that such a man as Con was standing just below the two flags that meant honor and loyalty. Con Adams was a man who served no flag nor anyone else other than himself.

The trail to Victor was almost five miles long from Cripple Creek. We passed more than a few gold miners either coming or going along the trail. They took no interest in Ghost or myself, but to the man they all kept a wary eye on Timber as they passed us or we passed them. We had no sign that anyone from the McPherson gang was following us or even watching us on the trail from a high vantage point.

Victor as a mining camp was not much to speak of. It was just a smaller brother of Cripple Creek. As we rode through the camp, just like in every camp and town so far, the children gathered behind us and followed Timber. Timber once again seemed to soak in all the attention he was receiving and seemed to pick up his strut as if he was some celebrity or something. Ghost saw it too and said to no one in particular, "That wolf's head is going to get so big we will never be able to get him through a saloon door ever again."

Smiling, I stopped Gypsy and looked down at the yellow-eyed wolf as he was also stopped and looking upward toward Ghost with an expression on his snout that seemed to say, "What the hell!"

Both Ghost and I laughed out loud as we once again headed southeast toward the mouth of Phantom Canyon. It wasn't long before we reached our destination. There was a large white boulder standing all by its lonesome on the west side of the trail just as the blonde-headed outlaw had mentioned back at the Imperial Saloon in Cripple Creek. Knowing we were probably being watched, we dismounted just as we had been told to do. I gathered the makings for a fire and started to make a small cook fire. Once the flames caught hold of the kindling, I asked Ghost, who had been studying the lay of the land, "Anything?"

Ghost nodded his head "yes," and replied, "I caught the flash of their binocular glass. There are still two watching us now down to the southwest in that clump of aspen trees. A third hightailed it into the canyon. I reckon it will not be long before Alistair McPherson or his brother Alban show up."

Standing up, I looked southwest toward the aspen trees and as I was doing so, Ghost stepped in front of me and reached out and handed me a dog-eared plain white envelope. Instinctively, I took it from him and he must have seen the confusion on my face as I spoke, "Eric Robert, sometimes in a man's life he knows he has no control over his fate - fate and destiny have led him down a certain trail in life that is preordained. This my friend is one of those times in my life. I know in my heart I was supposed to be here with you today to face these Scottish outlaws. I guess I would not have it any other way. Just know it is my honor to be here today to fight to bring your granddaughter home."

Looking my friend in the eye, I held the letter up and said with confusion in my voice, "It is my honor as well to ride this trail with you, Matt Lee. But, what is the letter for?"

Ghost returned my gaze eye-to-eye and speaking in a voice that was clear and with no hesitation, "It is a letter to Walk With Ghost. If this goes south for me here on this day, I want you to take it back to Redemption Valley and bury it with my wife."

Ghost had made his intentions clear and with his help and the Lord willing, I would be able to take my granddaughter back for those that held her for ransom. There was no gesture big or small I would not do for this man. Still with some confusion in my voice, "When did you write the letter, Matt?"

Ghost with no tears or sadness in his voice said, "The night after we talked to Connor's parents in Alma. Promise me for payment for what will happen here today, you will do me this favor."

Death comes to us all, and it is said some have the clout to see it heading their way just like a locomotive heading down the tracks. Others are just blindsided by it. It would seem that Matt Lee was one of those who has seen the signs of the specter of darkness in his future. If Matt Lee thought he needed to write and give me this letter, I for one was going to accept it. Reaching out with my hand, I grabbed the hand of the man who had been a foe and now was my best friend and shook it with all that I had to give. Speaking man to man to the legend known as Ghost, "I promise Matt."

Chapter 13

I thought about what was to come and then asked Ghost his thoughts, "How do you want to play it, Matt?"

Ghost did not hesitate and I could see in his eyes that killer instinct had taken hold of him, and it was this deadly trait that defines the legend and the man known as Ghost as he spoke, "We should be on horseback when facing so many. Your one and only goal is to get your granddaughter out of here as quickly as you can. I will protect the rear and take out as many as I can. Simple really, Marshal."

The plan was just that simple and probably the only plan that even had a remote chance of working. Violence and death were not strangers to men such as Matt Lee and myself or to those that held Connor for that matter. No different from fighting fire with fire when the forest is burning down the mountain toward your cabin. There would be no law here today other than that of the righteous. I knew someday I would have to face the Ole Mighty for things I had done in my past and for things I was about to do. If a seat in Hell was the answer for my sins committed then and now, I would gladly pay that price to see Connor safe.

Ghost and I both palmed our Colts and checked the loads. Having done that, we checked our Winchesters, and I checked my second scabbard that held my 12-gauge Greener shotgun loaded with double-ought buckshot. Pushing any fear of dying to the back of mind, I brought forward the warrior in me. Ghost and I were ready for Alistair and Alban McPherson and their outlaw brethren.

Sitting in my saddle on Gypsy with Spirit grazing nearby, watching the mouth of Phantom Canyon, I was getting antsy, and I fidgeted. Ghost looked calm and his demeanor seemed that of a man out on a casual ride for the day. Cimarron was as calm as his rider.

Timber was sitting, but his ears were standing straight up and he was not missing a thing. He might not know exactly what was going on, but there was no doubt he was as ready as he could be.

We sat in our saddles for another ten minutes when six men rode out from Phantom Canyon leading two extra horses. Even from these distances, on one horse I could make out the features of the young girl whose hands were tied to the saddle horn. I knew it to be my granddaughter Connor. She was the spitting image of her mother at that age. My heart skipped a beat just looking at her. On the second horse being led sat an older woman with long, dark brown hair. From this distance the woman had the look of a fair-skin Mexican or of Spanish heritage. Her hands also were tied and obviously was a prisoner of the Highlanders. Speaking to Ghost without looking at him I said, "We take the older woman as well!"

Ghost, without looking at me replied, "Already planned on it, Marshal!"

Leaving two men behind to guard Connor and the woman, four men separated and rode in our direction. Wanting to lessen the distance between Connor and myself, I gave Gypsy a slight jab with my right spur and headed her out to meet the four men. Timber's hair on his back stood straight, and I could feel the tension from the yellow-eyed wolf as he walked stride for stride along Cimarron. The rider in the front of the others had an air of authority and was obviously Alistair McPherson. Alistair had short brown hair and seemed at least thirty years younger than Ghost or myself. He was dressed just like any other ranch hand or cowboy that rode the Rocky Mountain frontier. As we got closer I asked Ghost without looking at him, "How many total?"

Ghost replied quickly, "Twelve total, the six in front of us; two still down in that aspen grove; four just beyond the evergreens; and fifty yards behind, your granddaughter and the other woman. I will engage those four riding to meet us and the ones down by the aspen grove when you go for your granddaughter. If I am still alive, I will battle those in the aspen grove and evergreens as you ride like hell to get your granddaughter and the other woman out of here safely. Promise me Marshal, that when we separate that no matter what happens, your priority is your granddaughter."

Matt Lee was correct in stating that getting Connor safe was the mission. I took a quick glance at Ghost before I replied. What I saw was a man who - with all the death and destruction that had happened in his life - had not lost what made him human. Deep in the chest of a legend known as Ghost beats the heart of a loving and caring man. Answering the legend in a clear and calm voice, "I promise!"

Ghost looked at me and when his eyes found mine, he said, "You are a good man, Eric Robert! Let's get your granddaughter and kill some Scottish outlaws!"

We had nothing to bargain with since we did not have the $100,000 ransom, so there would be no reason to even try to negotiate with Alistair McPherson. Ghost knew it and I knew it. When we were about forty yards from the four that had ridden out to meet us, I spurred Gypsy into a full out gallop as did Matt Lee with Cimarron. Ghost headed straight for the four in front of us as I peeled off and headed for those guarding Connor and the other woman. Out of the corner of my eye, I saw Ghost pull his Winchester and shoot the man on the far right of him out of his saddle.

As more gunfire erupted behind me, I raced on toward Connor. The two guards were so startled by the sudden frontal attack that they were slow to react and their horses were just as disconcerted and bucked tossing one outlaw violently to the ground. Palming my Colt and firing, I missed on the first round at the guard still mounted. My second round found its mark in the man's chest, and he went down hard.

Gypsy had closed the gap quickly, and I was pulling back on her reins as I came up on both Connor and the woman. The first guard that had been bucked off had by this time regained his feet and was reaching for his holstered pistol when I shot him twice, once in the throat and the follow up through the face. He was dead before his body hit the ground.

Holstering my pistol and almost in the same motion, I switched the reins to my other hand and then unsheathed my Bowie knife. Bringing Gypsy under control, I reached out and grabbed Connor's horse's reins and brought her horse under control, and I reached out and sliced through the rope that was binding her hands. Quickly moving toward the other woman, I did the same. Looking the woman in the eye, I said in a hurried voice, "How well can you ride?"

The woman's eyes were wide with the excitement of the moment and replied in an excited voice, "Like the wind!"

Pointing my Bowie Knife toward the trail heading toward Victor, I said in a loud and clear voice, "Take Connor and ride like hell in that direction, and I will be along shortly. Do not wait for me until you get to the Imperial Palace in Cripple Creek!"

Connor, by the way she had taken control of the outlaw horse, had skills as well. She had to yell over the gunfire and gunfight that was aimed at Ghost behind us, "Who are you?"

Still pointing with my Bowie, I had to yell over the increasing ruckus of the ongoing battle with the outlaws and Ghost, "I am your grandpa, Connor! Now ride!"

A smile split my young granddaughter's face as she spurred her horse into a full gallop, hollering over her shoulder as she rode away, "I KNEW IT!"

Making sure that Connor and the woman were well on their way, I sheathed my Bowie knife and then spun Gypsy around as I also reloaded my Colt to see how Ghost was making out. All the remaining outlaws, out of their instinct to save their boss, had converged on Ghost. During the assault on Alistair McPherson's position, Matt Lee had become dismounted when apparently Cimarron had been shot out from beneath him. Ghost was using the body of the famous horse as a bunker and shield as he waged war as only Ghost could wage war. The ground was littered with five dead or dying outlaws and three other horses thrashing about in their death throes.

Timber had taken down one horse and another was trying to stand, obviously hamstrung by the yellow-eyed white wolf. Timber in his all-out bid to save Matt Lee was keeping the remaining outlaws' horses in a panic as they bucked and tried to trample the wolf. Timber was swift and agile and was proving to be a mighty warrior, and he hamstrung another horse as the outlaws were throwing lead his way just as much as they were shooting at Matt Lee.

Matt Lee looked in my direction and even from this distance, I could see by his pained movement he had caught a bullet or two in the gunfire exchange. Seeing me, he pointed in the direction that Connor and the woman had fled. His meaning was loud and clear, "Get the hell out of here!"

With a feeling of remorse and guilt, I turned and spurred Gypsy in the direction that Connor and the Mexican woman had ridden. Making up 200 yards at a full gallop, I closed the distance between where my other horse Spirit had been left standing. Once I gathered up Spirit's reins, I spun once more toward the continuing gunfight between Ghost and the outlaws. My heart sank as the wounded legend was either out of ammunition or had not had enough time to reload during the battle as he stood on shaky legs and heaving lungs with his Bowie knife extended urging the outlaws to fight hand-to-hand. As Timber was still creating havoc with the other Highlanders gang's horses, Alistair McPherson split off from the rest that were battling Timber and calmly rode in Ghost's direction. With calm determination the still mounted Scottish outlaw fired twice into Matt Lee's chest.

Chapter 14

Instinctively, I touched the note in my vest pocket that Ghost had written for his wife and I knew he was gone. Knowing Ghost had given his life so my granddaughter had a chance to live hers did not quell the anguish I felt when I saw Alistair McPherson kill Matt Lee. Knowing now was not the time to avenge the Ghost's death, I quickly tied Spirit's reins to the back of my saddle and then spun both horses around and spurred Gypsy and gave her the reins and her head as we galloped toward Connor, the other woman and Victor, Colorado.

As Spirit was matching stride for stride with Gypsy, I deciphered the numbers in my head. Out of the twelve members of the Highlanders gang, I had killed two, and Ghost had killed or wounded five which brought the total down to five remaining. Alistair McPherson was one of those left alive, but I was not sure about his brother. The Highlander McPherson would not think kindly of not getting the $100,000 ransom and that Ghost and I killed or shot up more than half of his gang. There was no doubt that once he had gotten control of his gang and tallied up who was left that he would be in pursuit.

With Gypsy's build and fitness, she could maintain a full gallop longer than most horses so I let her run until I felt we had put considerable distance between the Highlanders and myself. After two miles I slowed Gypsy to a trot and spoke lovingly to her telling her she was the greatest horse and that she had done well in putting some distance between us and those that meant us harm. Gypsy tossed her head several times letting me know she had heard and appreciated my praise.

Moving through Victor, I kept a close eye out just in case Connor and the woman captive did not know the difference between Victor and Cripple Creek. I had no knowledge if my granddaughter or the older woman knew the territory they were riding in. Feeling confident they had moved on to Cripple Creek, I did as well.

Once entering the mining camp of Cripple Creek, I immediately made my way to the Imperial Saloon. I felt relief when I recognized the two horses that Connor and the captured woman had been riding at a horse trough filled with water across the roadway from the boardwalk to the Imperial Saloon. Dismounting at the same horse trough, I let Gypsy and Spirit get some much-needed water after their run from the mouth of Phantom Canyon. As I was getting the horses watered, I noticed one of the outlaw's horses that Connor and the woman had been riding was limping badly from its own run. Whoever had been riding that horse would now have to ride Spirit.

Even though I knew there was no way the outlaws could have gotten ahead of me to Cripple Creek, I checked the loads in my Colt. Once that was done, I headed over to the Imperial knowing time was burning and we needed to get out of town quickly before Alistair McPherson and the rest of the Highlanders gang showed up here looking for blood. Not just anyone's blood, but my blood.

Stepping through the Imperial's bat-wing doors, I was almost immediately swarmed by Connor as she flowed into my arms. I lowered myself in a half-squat to be the same height as Connor. With tears flowing and a voice that was cracking, she said, "Oh

Grandpa, I was so worried about you. Veronica said you would be along shortly, but I was so scared."

Holding Connor tightly, I reassured her that I was here for her. A tear formed in my eye. It had been longer than I could remember that I felt such a genuine love for another and it felt good to hold her. After several minutes I finally let go and gently separated from her and said, "We will have time to catch up later Connor, but for now I need to get a long look at you."

Holding Connor at arm's length, I looked at the young girl who was my only grandchild. She was small in stature even for a ten year old, but I could see her strength. She was the image of my daughter at the same age and had the eyes of green of her grandmother. Her hair was the color of a raven and long, almost to the center of her back. As I took a long look at her, Connor began to cry again...one of those cries of someone who had been through a long ordeal and thankful to be safe. Pulling her in again, I kissed her on top of her head and said, "Let it out Connor; let it all out."

The Imperial Saloon barkeep Randall and the four other patrons had all fallen silent as they witnessed Connor and my meeting for the very first time.

The woman whom I now knew as Veronica walked tentatively over and gently placed her hand on Connor's shoulder to offer support which only a woman could give. Looking up, I found Veronica's dark brown eyes and nodded my thanks to her. There was no doubt that this woman had been more than just another soul being held prisoner. I could feel the connection between Veronica and Connor...that bond of two people who had thought their situation was hopeless and needed each other's strength to endure. Holding Connor in my arms and Veronica's eyes with my own eyes, I spoke to Veronica, "My name is Eric Robert and as you gathered, I am Connor's grandpa."

Veronica was still caught up in the moment and the tears flowed. After a few seconds she finally found the strength to speak, "My name is Veronica Flores. I am so thankful and grateful for what you and that other gentleman did, Mr. Robert. The other man did he make it?"

Still holding Connor, I stood slowly and with my eyes locked on Veronica I nodded my head - no. Before Veronica could say anything I spoke, "That's not all Miss Flores; there are still five of the Highlander gang alive and there is no doubt they will be heading this way. I am not sure how you ended up as a prisoner of theirs, and we don't have the time to discuss it right now. You can stay here if you feel safe enough or you can go with us to Alma, Colorado. You need to decide right now because we need to put some distance in between Alistair McPherson and us."

Veronica did not even hesitate before she spoke, "I know time is of the essence, but you need to know Mr. Robert, that there is nothing here for me. If you will tolerate me, I shall be going to Alma with Connor and you."

By the smile on Connor's face, I could tell she liked the idea of having Veronica along. Connor broke my embrace and in turn embraced Veronica. The attachment that was formed with each other during the time they were being held captive was now an unbreakable bond. I was not so convinced it was a good thing that Miss Flores would accompany us and felt Veronica might be safer here. With no time to debate the right or wrong of the situation, I said, "Then we need to get on the trail!"

After pointing in the direction of the bat-wing doors that led to the outside, Connor and Veronica walked out onto the boardwalk. Just as I was going to make my exit, Randall the barkeep said, "Marshal Robert, I think you should know that Sheriff Adams wanted to know if and when you will return to Cripple Creek. It is my thought he is still fuming over how you made him back down yesterday."

Looking back toward Randall, I replied, "Much appreciated Randall. You are a good man and just know that you will always have a friend in me."

Stepping out onto the boardwalk, I surveyed the road in front looking for anyone who was more interested in me than they should have been. Connor and Veronica had already crossed the road and were standing next to Gypsy, Spirit, and the outlaws' horses by the horse trough. Just when I stepped off the last wooden step and touched the dirt of the road, Sheriff Con Adams appeared from behind an awning post on the other side of the street and stepped off onto the roadway as well. A confrontation with Con was the last thing I needed right now. Alistair McPherson and his remaining band of cutthroats would be here soon, and I didn't have time to deal with the likes of a pissed off sheriff. Con kept his eyes on me as he moved slowly to the middle of the street.

Veronica and Connor had both taken notice of the sheriff's movement, and they both had enough wherewithal to feel the tension now building between the Cripple Creek Sheriff and myself.

I hoped beyond hope that Con would just let me walk across the street and get mounted and ride out of Cripple Creek. Any beef or argument I had with the sheriff or he had with me could be settled at a later date.

Any faith I had in getting out of this mining camp peacefully was dashed when Con Adams said loudly and clearly, "I will be having words with you, Marshal Robert!"

Chapter 15

Turning to face the sheriff I said, "I don't have time for this Con! I need to get my granddaughter and Veronica back to Alma. If you want to follow me there, I will be more than happy to oblige you in any manner you want."

Con Adams spread his feet into a gunfighter's stance with his feet directly below his shoulders. His intention was perfectly clear as he replied in an unhurried voice, "You are not riding anywhere Marshal, but I promise to pay for your funeral."

I readied myself for what was to come. Speaking loudly, but still looking at Con, "Veronica, take Connor inside the store there behind you."

Veronica did not miss a beat, and she grabbed an almost in shock Connor by the shoulder and ushered her up the boardwalk steps and into the store. With Connor and Veronica now safe from catching a stray bullet, I focused on all that could affect the outcome of the impending duel with Con Adams. The sun was hidden behind a dark and cloudy autumn sky. The air was chilled but not cold enough to warrant gloves. I smelled the wetness of the mud mixed with the dirt road and I could feel the moisture on my face in the northern breeze. My eyes sharpened so I could see every aspect of Con's face and eyes even with the forty yard distance that separated us. I could see the dark stubble of the beginnings of a beard and his dark brown eyes were as focused as mine were. His gun rig was a shiny black leather holster with a well-cared for 44 Colt resting in its sheath with the grip pointed backwards for a standard draw. Con was as ready as he would ever be. So was I.

The younger man started his draw, but he did not have the speed or the experiences I had. Palming my Colt quickly, I landed my first bullet lower than I intended just above Con's belt buckle. My second bullet caught the dying sheriff in the chest just below his throat as his knees folded. Con Adams dropped his pistol in the dirt and mud of the road once his knees landed hard. Con's eyes were still looking in my direction, but they could no longer see as death overtook the man. Con was already dead as he finally collapsed onto the road face first - the same road in the same town that he was sworn to protect.

There were no feelings of anger, relief, triumph, or remorse. I had already spent my emotions of the day with the death of Matt Lee and possibly Timber. Since I had been so focused on Ghost, I did not pay attention to what may have happened to the yellow-eyed white wolf. My only thought was getting Connor, Veronica, and myself on the trail and putting some distance in between Alistair McPherson and those that rode for him. Getting Connor and Veronica to safety was the mission and right now that was in Alma, Colorado.

The boardwalks quickly filled with the townsfolk as they always do in the aftermath of a gunfight. Looking for Connor and Veronica, I saw them standing on the boardwalk as they were staring at me in disbelief of all that had happened today. I saw no honor in killing a man in front of my granddaughter, but it was something I could not have avoided. Con Adams pushed the fight, and he paid the ultimate price. Knowing I had lost some precious time in dealing with Con, I half expected Alistair McPherson and his men to come riding into the town of Cripple Creek. Pointing toward Gypsy, Spirit, and the other horses, I said to Connor and Veronica, "We got to go and I mean right now."

In quick fashion Veronica got settled into her saddle on the outlaw horse that was not lame. I helped Connor on to Matt Lee's and Walk With Ghost's horse Spirit. Once that was done, I squared myself into the saddle on Gypsy. Riding first north out of Cripple Creek for a mile, I decided on a different route to Alma and reined Gypsy almost due west. There was a new mining settlement that had sprung up on Freshwater Creek called Guffey. Alistair McPherson would assume I would take Connor back to her home using the most used trail to Alma and that would be to head north. To avoid a running gun battle with the Highlander, I decided that heading north first then west was the best option. If the outlaw gang happened to have a decent tracker, my plan was for naught.

After pushing the horses hard for the next two miles, I slowed Gypsy, Spirit, and the outlaw horse down to a pace they could sustain without faltering.

Connor, Veronica, and I rode in silence. We were all tired, hungry, and still overcome by the events of the day. The battle with the Highlanders and the rescue of Connor and Veronica, and the death of the famous mountain man Matt Lee weighed heavily on my mind. Ghost had given his life so Connor could live her life as she saw fit, and I would give my life as well to protect her. My mind drifted to Timber and wondered if his life was given as well in the quest to free Connor; my hope was after Ghost had been killed that Timber made his way into the trees and freedom. After the earlier shoot-out with the Highlanders, the gun fight with Con Adams seemed as if it almost had not happened even though he was left lying in the streets of Cripple Creek with two of my bullets in him. The day's events had happened quickly, and my fear was that they were not over by a long shot.

The day was getting shorter, and the clouds had gotten darker overhead and it looked as if a storm was brewing in the north. The air became colder to the point of seeing our horses' breath as well as our breath as it misted in the now damp air. We all needed food and a place to rest; I needed to find a campsite that would provide shelter from the incoming storm as well as a site that was hidden from the trail and the likes of Alistair McPherson and those I thought to be in pursuit.

Staying off the beaten and most traveled trail to Guffey, I kept us riding due west with Mount Pisgah just to the south of our traveling caravan. Hopefully if Alistair McPherson had figured out that we were indeed heading toward Guffey instead of straight north that by taking the high and the more difficult trail, we could hopefully lose them because they had poor woodcraft in tracking or they would just be plain lazy and would stick to the easier and lower trail. It was at this moment it dawned on me how much I missed Matt Lee and his mountain man skills. Touching the letter in my vest pocket Matt Lee had written his wife, I knew if and when I got Connor and Veronica to Alma that my next mission was to fulfill my promise to the legendary mountain man and that Redemption Valley would be my next destination.

Looking south, I could see that the storm had brought snow, and it was snowing two thousand feet above us on top of Mount Pisgah. Pisgah topped out just above timberline where the trees did not grow anymore because of those lofty heights. My gut was telling me that the autumn days and months were done for and the snow would travel down the mountainside within the next hour. The storm and snow could be our blessing, and I hoped it would cover our back trail and help us disappear from those that wanted to reclaim Veronica and Connor and most likely wanted me dead.

A half hour before sunset, I found the campsite I wanted, and it was high up on the mountain side just above the bank of Bernard Creek. Bernard Creek was a small creek, and it ran north and south and our campsite for the night had a thick stand of evergreen trees shielding us from the east and the north. It would be about as safe as I could hope for. I doubted that Alistair McPherson and his men would ride the rough terrain of the mountainside to the south of our location. And just as I thought it would, it began to snow; flakes as big as one dollar gold coins started floating back and forth in an easy arch from the sky.

I indicated with hand signals to Veronica and Connor that we would make camp here. Even though both were exhausted from the rescue and the gunfights of the day, they both dismounted quickly and began the chore of making camp. It made me proud to see Connor without my asking to gather firewood as Veronica gathered the stones to build a ring for the warming fire we would need tonight. Whilst I still had a few minutes of daylight, I caught

Veronica's eyes with my own and she understood I needed to check our back trail for pursuit. When I handed Veronica the 12-gauge Greener shotgun from my second scabbard, she took it like she knew how to use it and quickly broke it open to check if it was loaded. As soon as Veronica assured herself that it was, she snapped it closed and then nodded to me. Veronica Flores it would seem was one to ride the river with. Reining Gypsy around, I rode eastward for fifty yards back over the trail we had ridden on. Dismounting Gypsy, I pulled my lever action Winchester from its scabbard and took up a sentry post.

The snow was now falling almost straight down with little or no wind. Big fluffy and heavy flakes were starting to dust the needles of the evergreen trees and our back trail. If not for what had happened today, I would be at peace with all that surrounded me. The Rocky Mountains in all its glory of a new snowstorm were one of the most beautiful sights you could ever encounter.

Just as darkness prevailed over the mountains, I saw movement. I winced a tad when the sound of my levering my Winchester seemed to echo off the mountainside. Shouldering my rifle, I followed the movement with the rifle sight as it got closer. A grin split my face as I realized what the white flash of movement was.

Lowering the Winchester, I waited until Timber caught up with me. The yellow-eyed wolf, once he was five yards away, promptly sat his butt down and stared at me with his tongue hanging out in near exhaustion. Returning the wolf's gaze I said, "Damn Timber, you got one hell of a nose to track us down, but I am glad to see you!"

Chapter 16

As I looked at Timber, the yellow-eyed wolf seemed as if he had come through the battle with the Highlanders with no wounds or hindrances. As glad as I was to see him, it also saddened me because Timber reminded me that Matt Lee did not make it out of the fight alive. A flood of guilt ran over me knowing his body was still lying at the mouth of Phantom Canyon. The man known as Ghost knew what he was getting into and understood the consequences. Still didn't make it right. There was no other choice other than to keep moving until Connor and Veronica were safe. Knowing Alistair and Alban McPherson and the remaining members of his outlaw gang would be tracking me with a blood lust for revenge, I knew that it would be pure luck if we all came out of this alive.

Still keeping his distance as I was in thought, Timber had tilted his head as if he was wondering what the hold-up was. Grinning, I said, "Guess it is time you met the rest of the pack."

Timber waited patiently until I got mounted on Gypsy and then he matched Gypsy's stride for a stride on my right as we headed back to camp.

The smell of frying bacon danced on the air as I got closer to the camp. Darkness had fallen and as soon as I could see the orange glow of the campfire, I spoke into the night, "Veronica and Connor, I am coming in with a friend so don't shoot us!"

Approaching the fire while still mounted, I saw Veronica standing with the Greener shotgun at the ready, making sure I was alone and not being coerced by the Highlander outlaws. Seeing Timber and me all by our lonesome, she had a smile spread across her very beautiful face. She was obviously relieved, but I loved she was ready and willing to stand her ground. Veronica seemed to be the type that looks adversity and hardship in the eye and gives it a wink. There was no doubt that Veronica Flores was one hell of a woman.

Connor's face, while she had been eating bacon and beans, lit up as well and with a delightful voice, "Grandpa, you found your wolf. What's his name?"

At this moment, seeing Connor and Veronica by firelight with smiles as big as the sky, I was a happy man. Answering Connor, "His name is Timber. Just be aware he is not a tamed critter by any stretch of the means. He is wild as they come, so be wary of him."

Even before the words were finished coming out of my mouth, Timber made a beeline toward Connor. He was so quick in his movements toward my granddaughter that I palmed my Colt in anticipation of having to shoot the yellow-eyed cur. What happened next astonished me to no end. He stopped next to the log Connor was sitting on and to her enchantment, he lowered his head onto her lap to be petted. Connor did what every kid would do when a loving dog did what Timber had done, and she set down her plate and wrapped her arms around the wolf's neck and hugged him like there was no tomorrow. Connor was still hugging the beast when she looked at me with smiling eyes and said, "I like your wolf, grandpa!"

Since Timber had not chewed off Connor's arm, I slowly holstered my Colt and with the sound of astonishment in my voice, "Until this moment I thought Timber belonged to no one and sure as hell not me. I believe Connor is now your wolf."

Connor's eyes widened with shock and she asked, "Grandpa, you mean Timber is mine?"

Connor's innocence was so genuine it brought a chuckle from me as I answered her question, "I guess Timber is yours, Connor. Not that you really had a choice in the matter; I believe Timber did all the choosing."

As I was unsaddling Gypsy, the night cooled, and the snow got heavier, which I was thankful for. The night and the now deepening snow would cover our tracks and I was thinking we may have slipped away from those I thought to be pursuing us. With Gypsy and now Timber's extra eyes and sensitive nose, I thought we were relatively safe for tonight, anyway.

As I used my wooden curry comb to brush down Gypsy, I looked back toward the fire and Connor had cuddled up under one of my spare flannel blankets. Connor still had her arms wrapped around Timber under the blanket for body warmth, and they both were sound asleep. I was still astounded at how quickly Connor was able to tame the savage beast, but sure as I was standing here, Timber seemed to be as friendly as any house dog. It would seem that the yellow-eyed beast had found his forever home with my granddaughter. As I was still looking at Connor and Timber, my heart melted.

After finishing grooming Gypsy, I gave all the horses some grain and a pinch of sugar each for a treat. Taking care of those that took care of us, I heard my stomach growl, and it was now time to take care of me. Heading to the fire, Veronica handed me a plate of fried bacon and beans for my supper.

Veronica moved about in silence as she tidied up the camp and then checked on Connor in a motherly way. I got a good look at the woman I had only met this morning. It was obvious by her actions on this day she was a woman who could take care of herself even in these remote mountains. I had no doubt that if given the chance, and I was not here, she could take charge and get Connor back home safely to her folks in Alma. She was a tad younger than I was, and her dark brown hair was tied into one pigtail that fell about a foot below her shoulders. Veronica Flores was slender and small in stature. Most women her size were frail, but not Veronica; she moved with determination and had the grace of a dancer. She looked at me cautiously several times as she moved about, and her deep, dark brown eyes caught the flicker of the campfire light, and those stunning eyes stirred my blood. There was no doubt that Veronica Flores was a strong, independent and fine-looking woman.

As Veronica sat on a log next to the fire, enjoying its warmth, she poured herself a cup of coffee that had been boiling on the campfire. And then she set the cup down into the snow at her feet to cool it down before drinking it. Now that I had the time and out of curiosity, I asked her, "Miss Flores, it is none of my business, but you have the look of possibly Spanish or Mexican heritage. The name Flores if I am not mistaken means flowers in Spanish. Is Flores a married name?"

Veronica smiled as she looked at me before replying, "It is Marshal Robert, but also in a twist of fate it is also my maiden name. My father's ancestry hails back to the original Spanish conquistadors that explored and fought alongside the likes of the famous conquistadors Hernán Cortés who conquered the Aztec Empire and Francisco Pizarro who led the conquest of the Incan Empire. My mother's lineage hails from those conquered Aztecs. The Aztec women were originally taken as slaves for the Spanish, but over the years became partners in more ways than one with their conquerors. They eventually became Christians and were married in the Catholic Church. My father worked building the railroads in central Mexico when he met my mother. They fell in love and had nine children, and I am the oldest daughter. Flores is a very common Spanish name, and I eventually married a man with the same last name.

It would seem that the mixture of Spanish and Aztec blood created a very beautiful and fascinating woman. Veronica seemed pleasant and talkative, so I asked another question that I was wondering about, "Mrs. Flores If you don't mind another question I was wondering about is how you became to be a captive of the Highlander gang? If you do not want to talk about it, I will not ask it again."

With the snow still falling and glistening her dark brown hair, Veronica slowly picked up her coffee cup and placed her hand gingerly on the side testing to see if it had cooled enough to hold. Satisfied that it had, she took a sip and her stunning dark brown eyes found mine and there was a hint of a tear as she spoke, "You were correct earlier when being polite and calling me "Miss" instead of Mrs. It has been a long time since I have been called that, Mr. Robert. Not sure I will ever get used to that handle again, but it is accurate. My husband died of the fever not forty-five days ago. It pains me to think of it now, and I am not sure why I feel the need to tell you about it."

Veronica paused for a whole minute as she looked not at me, but inside of me with her searching brown eyes. Obviously, whatever she saw in me pleased her that I was no threat as her face showed the release of the tension of recent days and especially the strain of today that had been plaguing her. After taking another sip, she continued, "Not much to tell Marshal, the same old story of lost fortunes and heartache that one will hear up and down the Rocky Mountain frontier. My husband Alejandro Flores had a gold claim just south of Cripple Creek and had been doing well enough that he sent for me to join him from Mexico. I had only been here two weeks when he caught the fever and no matter how much I prayed, the Lord took him home to a better place. Alejandro was a good man and about as hard working as any man could be. Despite the cold and the hard ground, I used a pickax to dig his grave, and I buried him on the gold claim he had worked so hard on. I sold the claim and with that money and what little gold dust that was left over, I bought a return trip back to Mexico and it was my intention to stay with my sister. The stage finally came, and I said my final goodbyes to Alejandro and Cripple Creek and boarded for the return trip back to Mexico. The stage was held up and robbed four miles east of Cripple Creek by Alistair McPherson and his brother Alban and their band of outlaws. Along with stealing the Independence Gold Mine payroll, all the passengers were raided of their money and jewelry if they had any. Not only did they take what little money I had left, but they also kidnapped me to sell down south to Comancheros. The only thing that kept me here and safe from being sold into slavery was that they needed me to look after Connor until someone paid the ransom; then they would have shipped both of us south."

Veronica looked heavenward at the falling snow and then briefly her eyes followed some red-hot embers that had drifted up from the fire and floated lazily on the heat waves above the campfire before they cooled and turned black, drifting off into the darkness. A few seconds later she took another sip of coffee before she spoke again, "I sit here tonight a woman that has lost everything. My husband, my future, any money I had, and don't even own a decent coat to ward off the snow and the cold. Even with all that has happened in the last month, I am thankful for you Marshal Robert, for saving me from an unpleasant fate. For now, all I can do is live moment to moment."

After pondering what Veronica had said, it was difficult for me to say any comforting words because such words from me did not roll easily off my tongue, so I said nothing. Rolling out my bedroll, I gave her my heavy wool blanket for her to sleep in. As I tossed another couple of good-sized logs on the fire I said, "With any luck Alistair McPherson and his brother Alban have lost our trail and are headed north. We should be able to reach Guffey with no interference from them."

Veronica wrapped the blanket over her shoulder and she snuggled down in it, but she looked at me in a confused manner before she said, "You don't know, do you? Alban McPherson, Alistair's younger brother, was one of the men holding Connor and myself when you came to Phantom Canyon. He was the one that had gotten bucked off his horse when the shooting had started. Marshal Robert, you killed Alban McPherson!"

Chapter 17

The words "Marshal Robert, you killed Alban McPherson" took longer than it should to sink into my hard head. With the death of his younger brother by me, it meant any chance of Alistair McPherson riding away from pursuing us was not going to happen. Connor's rescue went from a bad business decision for McPherson to a kin-related blood feud. Somewhere down the trail Alistair would kill me or I would kill him. Now I had to get my mind right and focus on what needed to be done.

Looking into the darkness and the snow and since I no longer had any blankets since Connor and Veronica had all that I had, I turned up my collar and pulled my hat lower to help cover my ears. Not ideal, but I had slept in worse conditions.

Sitting close enough to the fire to gather in the heat, I glanced at Connor, and she seemed to be warm enough. The huge white wolf was probably putting off the heat of a steam locomotive. It comforted me to know he had taken a shine to my granddaughter, and I felt assured he would give his life to protect her. Seems fate had taken a hand here and brought my granddaughter another angel. First Veronica of mixed Spanish and Aztec Indian heritage and now Timber.

My thinker was running full speed trying to put all that had happened today into some semblance when Veronica stood up with the blanket wrapped around her shoulders. She first checked on Connor, and when she was satisfied my granddaughter was warm and sleeping soundly, she walked over to me. With the blanket still on her shoulders, she opened it wider and placed half of it around me as she lay down beside me. In a quiet tone as not to wake Connor, "Miss Flores, this may not be appropriate."

Veronica chuckled that sweet and sultry sound she had and then said, "The name is Veronica. I need the warmth as much as you do, so be quiet about it. It has been a long day and we both need sleep."

As the snow continued to fall, Veronica cuddled up to my back, and she said, "Goodnight, Marshal."

It would seem that not only was Veronica a strong and capable woman, but she also could be a tad pushy. I liked that. Clearing my voice before speaking, "Goodnight Veronica."

Waking up, I tried not to move and disturb Veronica. It had been a difficult day for her yesterday and she had been exhausted last night. Blinking my eyes to clear my sight, I then looked at the fire's flames dancing upon the aspen logs as they consumed the wood. That confused me since I did not recall getting up during the night and adding wood to the fire. Then the smell of roasting rabbit reached my nose, and I thought, "What the hell?" Then I heard the clunk of a dropping tin cup against the ring of stones lining the campfire, quickly followed by Veronica saying, "Shit!"

After reaching behind me to feel the ground where Veronica had been sleeping and finding it to be bare, I sat up and peeked over the top of the flames and saw sets of three different eyes looking at me – Veronica's, Connor's, and Timber's. I was almost ashamed that all three had woken up before me. I was not accustomed to being the last one up. Sheepishly in a voice still not awakened from sleep I said, "Good morning."

That set Connor in motion and she quickly stood up and sped around the campfire, literally jumping into my arms and hugging me. Smiling, Connor said with a voice of innocence, "Grandpa, I love Timber and thank you for giving him to me. Timber left in the middle of the night twice and brought back two rabbits. And they were already dead and not chewed up or anything. Veronica skinned and cleaned them, and we are having rabbit for breakfast. Isn't Timber the best wolf?"

As I was holding Connor in my arms, my eyes adjusted and I could see Timber not three feet away behind Connor. He had followed her when she had flowed into my arms, but now was keeping his distance watching over her. Timber the yellow-eyed white wolf to my delight had become Connor's protector. As I pulled Connor gently out far enough so I could look into her eyes, I felt just as I did way back when her mother was this age. Even though I had only met my granddaughter just yesterday, it felt as if I had known her for all my entire life. My heart skipped a beat or two and reminded me what love was all about. Just like Timber, there was nothing I would not do for this young girl - even giving my life to save hers. Remembering Connor had asked a question, I answered her, "Timber is the best wolf I have ever known, Connor. He has sure taken a shine to you, which is a good thing."

Veronica appeared holding two steaming plates of roasted rabbit and fried beans, one for me and one for Connor. After moving Connor to a better position for eating, we both took our plates, and I looked into Veronica's alluring dark eyes and said, "Thanks Veronica; it smells delightful."

Veronica chuckled her Veronica laugh and said, "Well, if I was you Marshal, I would not get used to having breakfast in bed. That is only reserved for the morning after you save two damsels in distress!"

Connor laughed out loud as did I. Still looking at Veronica and not trying to stare and give up my attraction I felt for her, I finally said, "Fair enough Veronica, and duly noted."

Timber left for a short time and then returned with another rabbit for his own breakfast. It was turning out that the white wolf had more manners and was more like a caring person than most folks I knew. It would seem that Timber was in this for the long haul. The only drawback was each time I looked at him, it reminded me of Matt Lee and the ultimate sacrifice he had given so Connor could live. Remembering my promise to the Rocky Mountain frontier legend and touching my vest pocket, I reassured myself that Ghost's last letter written to his wife Walk With Ghost was still there.

Getting the three horses ready had been a slight chore since during the night almost four inches of snow had fallen and had blanketed all the saddles and gear. The air was still chilled, and the evergreen needles had an icy frost to them this morning. The aspen trees within sight had lost all of their leaves during the night, bringing the end of autumn. Winter always came early in the high country and this year was no different.

As Veronica finished cleaning our camp, Connor helped me as best she could with the saddles, halters, and reins. Timber stood off keeping a close eye on Connor. He seemed to know what my granddaughter was all about. It still amazed me how quickly the two of them had become an inseparable pair. Actually, it was inspiring.

Since we had not the time yesterday, I introduced Connor to the horses - first my horse Gypsy and then Spirit. I took a few minutes to tell Connor about Spirit's former owners - the legend Matt Lee and his wife Walk With Ghost - so she could fully appreciate the man known as Ghost and what he did for her rescue. Not sure if Connor understood all of what I told her about Ghost, but someday she would fully comprehend what had happened. When we finally got to the outlaw horse, I realized I had no idea what this horse's name was. So in the spirit of this day, I let Connor do the renaming of the dapple gray mare. The name Connor chose was fitting enough and from this day forward the horse would forever be known as "Outlaw."

As Veronica and Connor got mounted, I thought about the trail ahead and what to expect. By midday if all went well, we would make Guffey. From the new mining camp and by my reckoning, it was another fifty-five miles to the northwest to the town of Alma and Connor's folks and the other grandpa. It was a lot of miles looking past the horizon and over my shoulder for the likes of Alistair McPherson and his bunch.

Giving Gypsy some rein and her head and a slight nudge with my right spur, we headed due west. Gypsy and I were in the lead, followed by Connor on Spirit, and then Veronica riding Outlaw. Timber, just like the good and dependable soldier he was, brought up the rear. With no prompting from me, it seemed Timber knew exactly what to do.

We finally made the outskirts of Guffey about midday. The snow hampered us some, so we had to tread lightly to keep the horses from sliding on the now muddy and slushy trail as the snow melted when the sun had broken through the clouds at sunrise.

Stopping about a half mile out, I studied the mining camp of Guffey with my field binoculars looking for any sign that possibly the Highlander gang had come this way and might have made it here before us. The town seemed peaceful enough with the locals going about their chores and daily business. Palming my Colt, I checked to see it was loaded with a full six and then holstered my pistol, leaving off the rawhide thong that prevented it from slipping out on the trail. After checking that my Winchester was also fully loaded, only then did I feel ready to ride on in.

Guffey, Colorado was the center of activity in the Freshwater mining district. Copper, silver, and gold were the dream of many that mined hereabouts. There also were several large cattle operations near the town as well.

The first order of business was to get Veronica and Connor outfitted properly for the cold, so we headed to the dry goods store, named of all things, Guffey Dry Goods. After tying off Gypsy, Spirit, and Outlaw to the hitching rail out in front, I gave the store clerk instructions to get the girls outfitted and a list of supplies needed that included two more blankets for the trail. Veronica, with all the pride of her upbringing and heritage, tried to object. I shushed her and pointed her back toward the clerk who was already finding a pair of Levi jeans that would fit Connor. Veronica huffed a bit, but she went ahead and looked for some better winter gear for herself.

Timber stood guard at the hitching rail and just like every town he had been in, he drew a crowd of youngsters that had never seen a wolf up close. I stood inside looking out of the broad glass window keeping an eye on Timber and the main road of Guffey. I needed to make sure no kids got too close to Timber since I feared for their safety just in case the white wolf did not find them as agreeable as he had Connor. The second reason was to look for anyone that might take a keener interest in us than they should - like the members of the Highlander gang. To my relief the local kids kept their distance from Timber; it would seem that they knew by instinct he was still a wild animal.

After about a half hour of the girls shopping, a man entered Guffey from the east riding a white and tan Mustang. As the new stranger got closer, I saw he was a lean fellow with a hawkish face and nose. He was wearing a dark duster and an almost new black cowboy hat. He also wore a two gun rig on his hips with the grips forward like he fancied himself a gunman. As soon as he saw the new horse Outlaw, he stopped and stared for more seconds than it took admiring a fine-looking horse. This man knew the horse... which was not good. Without taking my eyes off the man still on horseback, I called to the back of the room, "Veronica, could you step up here for a moment? I got someone I need you to look at."

Veronica walked up all smiles and strutting her new heavy flannel shirt that did nothing at all to hide her womanly figure beneath it. When Veronica had come to the window, I pointed outside to the man on horseback and asked her, "Do you know who that man is?" Without trying to be noticeable while Veronica studied the man on horseback, I could not stop myself from admiring the beauty of the woman standing next to me.

Veronica's smile evaporated as she saw the man mounted on the Mustang. "Yes, I do Marshal, That is John Hansen and he is one of the Highlander outlaws."

Two things were obvious. One, Alistair McPherson and his men had lost our trail yesterday. Two, he had also sent a scout in this direction.

Chapter 18

Connor joined us at the window as we looked out at John Hansen, and her smile disappeared. In a childlike worried voice, "Grandpa, will the man try to hurt Timber?"

Touching Connor's shoulder to reassure her, I said, "Not if I can help it Connor, not on my watch anyway!"

It puzzled the store keep when I asked everyone to step away from the windows, but he followed suit when Veronica and Connor stepped back further into the room. Once I was satisfied that all were as safe as they could be, I glanced once more out the window, and Hansen had dismounted and walked closer to get a better look at the horse we now called Outlaw.

As he approached Outlaw, Timber still next to the hitching rail guarding the horses, stood and took a menacing stance with his hackles raised on his back. Timber did not growl or make any sound, but his displeasure with John Hansen was on display for all to see. That stopped Hansen dead in his tracks as he was now confronted by the yellow-eyed wolf. His knees bent in such a way as if he was deciding whether to pull his Colt to shoot Timber. Stepping out onto the boardwalk in front of the dry goods store, I said in a loud and clear voice so there was no misunderstanding, "Mister that is my granddaughter's wolf and if you shot him, she would be upset. I don't like it when my granddaughter gets upset!"

Hansen glanced my way and then returned his gaze to Timber when he said, "Then call that white cur off before I ventilate it!"

John Hansen, if he realized it or not, was situated badly in this growing encounter. He was faced with two threats with Timber and myself. Hansen did not know how Timber would react nor did I. The other thing was once Hansen had dismounted his horse and I had walked out onto the boardwalk, it gave me the high ground. It was easier and quicker to draw and shoot lower than it was to draw and shoot higher because the arc of your draw was just a tad shorter. Pushing the advantage and keeping Hansen distracted by Timber I replied, "I figure you didn't hear me when I said that was my granddaughter's wolf. Timber barely tolerates me and he sure as hell doesn't listen to me. I am just as curious if he is going to chew off your arm as you are."

It was dawning on Hansen that he was in a precarious situation and the outcome would not be in his favor. Slowly he backed up toward his horse and further away from Timber. As he did so, Timber's hackles relaxed and lay back down. The white wolf then tilted his head to look at me as if he was asking if it was okay to stand down. I nodded my head toward the wolf in understanding that for now it was up to me about what happened next. There was only one way this would play out and there was no way I was going to let Hansen ride out of here today. He made his choice the day he decided to ride with the McPhersons. To ride with the likes of the Highlander gang, you became a thief, killer, and a man who would and had defiled women. Men like Hansen and those he rode with had sold women into bondage, slavery, and prostitution. And John Hansen and the others did not get a pass for killing my friend Matt Lee or kidnapping my granddaughter for ransom. Still speaking in a loud and clear voice, "The girls tell me your name is John Hansen and you know John, I will not let you ride out of here. No one kills a good man and a friend of mine and kidnaps my granddaughter and walks away."

John Hansen forgot about Timber since the wolf no longer seemed threatening and focused in on me after my not so veiled threat sank in. Hansen squared his feet underneath his shoulders in the classic gunfighter stance as he faced me. It was obvious the man fancied himself a gunfighter and in a confident voice, "Who are you again Mister? I mean other than a dead man walking!"

Having been in many such confrontations such as this, I had no fear. Leery of course, because this gunfighter was unknown to me, which did not make him any slower with his six guns. Men such as Lucas Eldridge, Chance Bondurant, Mac Patton, and Johnny Ringo were all unknowns at the beginning. My biggest advantage was I did not fear death; I knew at some time it would seek me out and embrace me. It was not if death would extinguish my life; it was just a matter of when. It was fate and fate only that brought one's death. Knowing this, I did not fear it since it was out of my hands. Hansen's question needed an answer. "Sorry, thought you already knew, but it seems you are a tad slow in the thinking department. My name is Eric Robert, and the young girl you kidnapped was my granddaughter."

A look of concern and then confusion flooded across the face of the gunman before he spoke, "Eric Robert? As in Marshal Eric Robert? We thought the grandpa was the wealthy gold mine owner in Alma."

John Hansen was distracted with the ins and outs of possibly kidnapping the wrong girl for ransom. The McPhersons and Hansen thought a wealthy mine owner was easy pickings for a ransom and double cross; they had not counted on a lawman bent on justice and revenge for taking his granddaughter. Matt Lee and I had surprised them at Phantom Canyon when Ghost and I shot up and killed more than half of their gang. Now that Hansen knew who he was in fact dealing with, several beads of sweat appeared on his forehead even though the temperature was cool. John Hansen, gunfighter wannabe, never had the upper hand here and now he knows it for a fact. I let the man sweat for a few seconds before I spoke, "Yes, Mr. Hansen - Marshal Eric Robert. I am the other grandpa. That grandpa in Alma has the gold, but I only carry lead for those that threaten what is mine. You might have noticed I am not sporting a badge because when the likes of those Scottish assholes and yourself kidnapped someone that is my kin, the law has no place in what I will do to bring her back and to kill those involved. There will be no trial, no judge, just justice at the end of a smoking barrel. So I ask you Mr. Hansen, how lucky do you feel today?"

This outlaw scout sent out to locate Veronica, Connor, and myself would not be returning today...or any day. John Hansen was fast, I had to give him that, but not fast enough. He pulled both Colts and got one shot off each that buried themselves into the mud and snow of the roadway four feet in front of the dying gunfighter. My first bullet caught him six inches below his throat and my second bullet caught him square in the teeth as he went down. Life when you are an outlaw ended just this way or at the end of a hangman's noose. It was the final judgment for living a life taking from others. It was the way it was supposed to be.

Stepping off the boardwalk, I walked over to the body of John Hansen and looking down at the man I had just killed, and there was no joy or remorse in killing this man. I felt justified in doing so, but it did not please me.

Veronica and Connor walked slowly out of the dry goods store and stood next to Timber. A crowd formed silently on both sides of the street as the folks of Guffey were drawn to the event of the day. Just like any other town or shooting I had seen or had been involved with, the town folks gathered out of morbid curiosity. Sometimes a shootout such as this will be told and retold for years after the occurrence.

Just as I knew it would happen, the man with the tin star and the sheriff of Guffey finally showed up on the boardwalk on the west side of the roadway. Jeffrey Simpson was known to me and seemed to be a good and fair man. He was probably thirty years younger than I was, and his head was shaved bald. His dark brown mustache was unkempt and shaggy to the point I could not see his lips move when he spoke. To the best of my knowledge, he had never been in a gunfight and I had never heard of his ability with the Colt pistol he carried on his right hip in a dark-tanned leather holster. I was hoping today was not the day he tried to test his quickness with his sidearm. I did not want to kill a noble man for doing his job, nor did I have the time to waste waiting out in jail for a trial for justice to be served. Sometimes the law worked in slow and mysterious ways, and my mission was to get Connor home safe as quickly as I could. The only place I was going today was north towards Alma.

Jeffrey stepped into the street and I could see his eyes. They were tough to read. One thing that was for sure was there was no fear in the young sheriff's eyes. When Sheriff Simpson got to within thirty feet of me, he stopped and pointed at the dead outlaw at my feet and said, "It would seem Marshal Robert, we have a misunderstanding here today!"

Chapter 19

Looking Sheriff Simpson in the eye, I replied, "No misunderstanding, sheriff. This man John Hansen was part of the Highlander gang and they kidnapped my granddaughter for ransom. He got paid in full."

The sheriff looked as if he was pondering my answer when he said, "I just got done reading a wire stating that you also had a misunderstanding in Cripple Creek yesterday morning with Con Adams."

It would seem that word traveled the telegraph wire faster than I could ride. Stating in a voice that was calm, "Sheriff Simpson, that was a misunderstanding on Con Adams' end. It would seem Sheriff Adams was under the impression that he was above the law for letting Alistair McPherson and his outlaws ply their trade in his jurisdiction. I disagreed with him. You probably will get another wire of seven more of the Highlander gang that are shot up or dead at the mouth of Phantom Canyon. Another misunderstanding from the McPherson gang for kidnapping my granddaughter."

Sheriff Jeffrey Simpson's brown eyes widened as he was doing the math. In a voice full of wonder and admiration he asked, "You have been busy, Eric Robert! You did all that by yourself?"

By his stature and demeanor, the sheriff was now showing he would not press the death of the outlaw John Hansen in his town any further. Now he was just curious about what happened. Bending down, I picked up Hansen's Colt pistols and walked the thirty feet distance in between Jeffrey Simpson and myself and handed the pistol grips first to the sheriff before I spoke, "I had help. Matt Lee gave his life at Phantom Canyon so my granddaughter could live hers. It is my intention that Matt did not die in vain, and no one will stand in my way getting Connor back home safe."

Sheriff Simpson's eyes widened even further when hearing Matt Lee's name. He spoke in a surprised voice, "Matt Lee? The same Matt Lee who was the legendary mountain man, the one they called Ghost? I thought he had died about a year ago; that was the rumor."

The memory of Alistair McPherson riding up and shooting Matt Lee in the chest twice flooded my vision, and I had to blink twice to clear my thoughts before responding, "One and the same. The rumor of his death was just that. He died yesterday in a noble effort to help me and my family. After Connor is home and safe, Alistair McPherson will have to answer for the death of my friend as well!"

After Jeffrey had taken the Colt pistols I handed him, he said in a lower voice so only I could hear, "Eric, you have done more for law and order of this state in the last day than most do in a lifetime. Con Adams was a corrupt official, and Cripple Creek will be better off without him. I salute you in all you have done and wish you Godspeed in getting your granddaughter home safely. Don't worry about anything here about Mr. Hansen; it would seem this was a lawful killing. The town will sell Mr. Hansen's belongings to pay for the undertaker and funeral. You are free to go."

Shaking the young sheriff's hand, I returned to the dry goods store and paid for all the purchases in full. Once the supplies and such were packed away on the horses, I helped Veronica and Connor get mounted before I planted my butt into my saddle. Timber gave me a sideways glance as if he was trying to tell me it was time to move back into the wilderness and put this town and the bad memories behind us. The white wolf said more than most folks I knew with just a gaze from his yellow eyes. Giving Gypsy her head and some reins, we started out of Guffey to the northwest following along the banks of Freshwater Creek.

Connor and Veronica had not said a word since the gunfight with the outlaw John Hansen which suited me just fine. Taking a man's life and everything he ever will be is not something I was proud of, and I needed time to get my mind right. My life had seen so much violence and death that at night I saw the faces of those in my dreams where I had a hand in how they died. The ghostly images of dead and dying men stirred my sleep on more occasions than I would like to admit. Some that worked the same side of the law as I do see themselves as an instrument of the Lord, and I had difficulty with that. They have always taught me the Lord worked in mysterious ways, but taking a life seemed a strange way to do his blessing. Most that are marshals and sheriffs at one time rode the outlaw trail and were just one hardship away from riding that trail once again. Taking someone's life in a lawful and righteous way may not be the ticket to heaven some might think. The day of my final judgment may give me a seat at the Lord's table or a seat in hell. My thought was it was a gamble either way - it could turn out my roll of the dice of life may come up snake eyes.

At noon we stopped just long enough so Connor, Veronica, and I could eat venison jerky and hardtack I had bought in Guffey. Not the most pleasant of meals but would have to do until I found a suitable campsite for the evening. I did not think Alistair McPherson had found our trail as of yet. It would not be long before he ended up in Guffey when his outlaw scout John Hansen did not return and then he would know for certain in which direction we were headed. With that thought in mind, I reined Gypsy due west leaving behind Freshwater Creek to locate Current Creek several miles west and then following it northwest to its headwaters at the base of Current Creek Pass. A little zig and a little zag could only help in confusing anyone in pursuit.

The trail before us, because of the recent snow, was sloppy and muddy, which made it almost impossible to hide three horses' tracks. I did my best by riding any hard granite when it made itself available. If any of the outlaws had half of the woodland tracking skills that Ghost had, the trail would be visible and any attempt on my part to hide the tracks would be for naught.

By mid-afternoon we located Current Creek and then continued north towards Alma. Just as before, I was in the lead, Connor behind me, and then Veronica with Timber bringing up the rear guard. The air had warmed during the day, but as the sun fell behind the mountains to the west, the temperature plummeted as well. With a cold evening in front of us, I felt relief that the girls were outfitted properly for the weather. Finally, I found a campsite that gave us protection from the wind, water from the creek, and off the beaten trail enough that hopefully anyone coming or going in the same direction would bypass us in the dark without knowing we were there.

Even though Connor, Veronica, and I had only been trail mates for a short spell, we had fallen into chores that benefited us all. My chore was to see to the horses and make sure they were pampered and fed and given a treat of sugar each day. Connor went about gathering stones and wood for our cook fire. Veronica made ready to prepare our supper for the night, which was a simple affair of bacon and beans and campfire tortillas. Timber provided security and moved about with his ears perked in the air listening and sniffing the wind for any signs of trouble while never getting too far from Connor. Timber somehow instinctively knew this ordeal the last several weeks was about Connor and he has become her protector. There was no doubt in my mind by Timber's reaction that my granddaughter was truly an angel. Just like Timber, I loved that little girl like no one else.

After supper Veronica and Connor quickly fell asleep, but I had trouble sleeping as the events of the last several days had been rolling through my mind. Connor had fallen asleep under her new blanket with Timber.

In the far distance, a wolf started to howl toward the heavens. Timber woke out of his slumber and carefully stood as not to disturb Connor and looked toward the darkness in the north. The howl in the distance was beautiful, eerie, and had a sense of loneliness in it. Watching Timber and his reaction to the kindred heart in the woods, I could sense his longing to follow suit and howl and join those that were of his kind. The howl was beckoning to the wild and savage side of the white wolf, but I knew he was where he wanted to be - here with us…with Connor. The faraway wolf howled one more time, and I could relate to what Timber was feeling of the wilderness. The Rocky Mountains cast a magical spell and held one in its net of wonder forever.

Not long after the last distant howl, Timber settled down with Connor and fell back into a deep sleep. Not long afterwards, I did the same.

Chapter 20

Waking up during the night when the almost full moon was directly overhead in a cloudless and starry sky, I watched Veronica stand and add wood to the nearly extinguished fire. With a long tree limb, she bent over and poked the fire to coax it back to life. In the orange hue of the dying fire, I could make out Veronica's face and her beauty mesmerized me. The Spanish and Aztec mix of her bloodline gave her an exotic look that at a different time or setting, wars would have been fought over such a woman. In the last couple of days, Veronica had proven to be a woman that most men longed for in their lives. She was capable, strong, and intelligent with the heart of an angel; her dark hued eyes and beauty rounded out the perfect companion. When she got home to Mexico and the local bachelors found out she was a widow, there was no doubt that they would trip over each other to court her. It was my intention not only to make sure Connor got to Alma safely but also that Veronica got back to her home. She deserved that and much, much more.

It was not long until the fire caught hold of the new logs and started their dance that consumed the wood that gave them life. Still watching Veronica from under the brim of my hat I had pulled over my eyes, I thought the position of my hat and with the darkness that she could not see me watching her. I was wrong. She turned her head and looked directly into my eyes and with a smile said, "I feel you watching me, Marshal."

Not knowing what to say I said nothing. Veronica smiled and then turned her gaze skyward saying, "It is so beautiful here and I can almost reach out and touch the stars. The moon seems to be just out of reach here; I never noticed that back in Mexico and I wonder why that is?"

Pulling back my hat, I sat up still facing Veronica and followed her eyes heavenward, speaking to her in an almost whisper as to not wake Timber and Connor. "That is because here you are so much closer to them. The cold air seems to bring more crystal clarity. The Rocky Mountains bring you high enough to touch the sky and even on some cloudy nights, you are higher than the clouds themselves especially above timberline. Here in the high country, I like the night, for without the darkness you would never see the moon or the stars. As a youngster, it was on nights such as this that I learned not to fear the night because I became too fond of looking at the starlight and the heavens. The moon and the stars in some way have become my friends - although silent - but nevertheless, my friends."

Veronica watched me as I spoke and was silent for a whole minute after I finished talking. "You are an interesting man, Eric Robert. You have the actions and demeanor of a predator, but your heart and soul sing a joyful tune. Simple and complicated; predator and prey; all wrapped up in the man known as Eric Robert."

Thinking about what Veronica had said, I replied with a chuckle, "Not sure what all that means, Miss Flores, but I think it was good. I am just a man with a set of morals and values I try to live up to. My code of ethics not everyone agrees with, but I am who I am."

Veronica stood over me and then said, "Connor has the heat box named Timber for warmth. Not sure about you Marshal, but I am cold and I would like to share your blanket again."

I opened my blanket and Veronica slid in and found a comfortable spot and immediately I could feel her body warmth and it felt good - very good. When I rolled over to face away from her, she cuddled up even closer and within a few minutes she had fallen asleep. It had been more years than I could remember when I had been in such close quarters with a woman, especially a beautiful woman, so sleep for me was a little tougher to come by. One thing I knew was that it felt good having Veronica next to me sharing my blanket.

Waking up this time before sunrise and before Veronica or Connor, I stood slowly as not to wake Veronica and poked the dying orange embers and glowing ash into a sizeable flame. Adding more wood, I waited until it took hold, and then I reached out my hands over the fire and felt the cold tingle of my fingers slowly disappear. Looking over at Connor, I realized Timber was already awake and had disappeared into the darkness of the new day. Maybe he had changed his mind and went to be with that wolf we heard last night. If he did, I couldn't blame him, but it would devastate Connor. For her sake, I hope he went to hunt up some breakfast for himself.

Timber returned twice before sunup, once with a big fat juicy rabbit, and once with a squirrel. The white wolf had seemed to take it as his responsibility to supply us with food, I had never heard of a wolf acting in such a manner. Timber was turning out to be not an ordinary wolf by any stretch of the means. I cleaned both of Timber's kills, and after Veronica woke up, she made a breakfast of roasted rabbit and squirrel with some fried beans and left over campfire tortillas.

Connor woke just as the sky was starting to turn orange with the new sun. Connor and Veronica were all smiles this morning and laughing and joking with each other, and I could not help but wonder what it would be like to have a full family with me each and every day. It would seem that having them here with me was more pleasing than I ever thought it would be. If not for the fact we were on the run from the Highlander gang this time, this moment was just about the finest it could ever be.

After getting Gypsy, Spirit, and Outlaw ready, we dismantled the campsite and did our best to erase any sign we had been here. Reining Gypsy in a northwest direction, we followed closely to the east side of Current Creek. The trail was still mushy from the recent storm and just above freezing temperatures. The sky was cloudless, and the day was turning out to be a typical Rocky Mountain early winter day.

At midday we stopped for a short time to eat venison jerky and hardtack and as the day progressed, my gut feeling was that Alistair McPherson and the other remaining four outlaws had either lost our trail or they were so far behind they had no chance of catching up with us prior to reaching Alma. I had to consider that McPherson would forget about trailing us and just head to Alma and if that was the case, I still had to get there ahead of him. In Alma I would have help from the local sheriff and the armed guards that Finn O'Brien had on his payroll to protect Connor. Most mine owners I had run across before had a small army of men at their disposal.

Despite the muddy trail conditions, we made good time and the base of Current Creek Pass by midafternoon. Current Creek Pass, as far as passes went, was not much to talk about. It topped out at 1500 feet below timberline and the slope was not bad for traveling on horseback. The only notable thing about the pass was that it was a boundary in between the Arkansas River Basin and the Platte River Basin. Since it was getting late in the day, I knew if we continued on we would have to make camp on top of the pass because of the encroaching darkness, so I opted to make camp at the base. This time of the year the higher up you are, the colder it got at night. I found a suitable campsite that gave us shelter from the wind by a stand of evergreens on three sides and a twelve foot high shelf of granite hard rock on the remaining side. The headwaters and the beginning of Current Creek was just a couple of inches wide and flowed directly from the ground not a foot away from where we had situated our campfire for the night.

Once again, I took care of the horses and got them ready for the night as the girls got the campsite ready and a fire going for our supper.

After a filling supper of bacon and beans, I produced two cans of peaches I had bought in Guffey for dessert. The girls seemed to enjoy the sweet treat as much as I did. Timber did as was his custom; he lay down at Connor's feet as the girls ignored me completely, taking turns talking about books they had read or wanted to read. Veronica's and Connor's experience together as captives of the McPhersons had created an unbreakable bond between the two. It was enjoyable to be an outsider of such conversations and watch the two of them as they laughed and smiled as they enjoyed each other's company.

I was sitting on a log on the opposite side of the fire from Connor and Veronica. Connor was the closest to the hard rock granite shelf. The rock soaked in the fire's heat and reflected it back so Connor had the warmest seat of the campsite.

Thinking about the days ahead, I became lost in thought and was lazily watching the red and orange dying embers as they danced in the heat above the campfire, slowly rising, then cooling, and then turning to ash as they floated away. Watching one very large ember take flight, I was curious how high it would reach, and before it turned to grey ash, I spotted just beyond it and at the top of the granite shelf just above Connor the unmistakable yellowish-green night eyes of a full-grown mountain lion.

Chapter 21

The comfort of the warming fire, the crisp and clear mountain air, and the feeling of family had all made me lazy. I had let my guard down slightly and was slow to react when the mountain lion sprang from the granite shelf intending to take Connor. Timber was not as slow.

The white wolf with his hackles raised met the lion in mid-flight as he moved to protect Connor from the sharp teeth and claws of certain death. Timber's weight and momentum had taken the lion off its path toward Connor, and they landed five feet to the west of my granddaughter. Connor and Veronica took several seconds to recover from the initial shock of the attack, but once recovered, moved swiftly out of the way and behind me as the two Rocky Mountain predators' life and death battle begun. Veronica grabbed my Winchester and jacked a round into the chamber - Veronica once again had proven she was one to ride the river with.

Having finally palmed my Colt, I held shooting out of fear of hitting Timber. Timber had the full-grown male lion's throat within his jaws and was savagely trying to rip the jugular out of the beast. The mountain lion was not going without a fight as the white wolf pinned the lion to the ground on his back. Blood flowed from the slashing and gashing grip that Timber had on the lion's throat; the lion in a desperate bid for its own survival slashed with its deadly claws at the underbelly of the yellow-eyed wolf. Even with its throat in Timber's violent back and forth shaking, the lion somehow gained his footing then lost it again. Back and forth; white and tan fur; blood, mud and snow; the mountain brutes rolled ferociously back and forth in this fight to the death. Timber had the advantage still gripping the jugular. As long as the lion could not get a good clasp with its claws on Timber's exposed belly and gut him in an unrestrained thrust, Timber would be in control. Even though it seemed forever, the fight between two of the Rocky Mountain titans lasted less than a minute. Timber finally with one last fierce thrust and tug did what I thought would never have been possible and bested the lion. With the lion in its dying spasms at the yellow-eyed wolf's paws and with its jugular torn from his throat, Timber stood victorious on shaky legs. Timber dropped the bloody lion's throat and raised his head to the heavens and the moon and howled his hauntingly and beastly sound of victory. With his triumph declared and with heaving lungs, he turned his head toward us and promptly collapsed.

Timber's snow white fur was matted with snow, mud, and blood. Connor, Veronica, and I rushed to Timber as his lungs were beating against his ribs as he tried to breathe. Connor with a few tears, but with a voice of strength, "Grandpa will Timber die?"

Placing Connor's hand on Timber's head, I indicated for her to pet him. "Connor, keep looking Timber in the eye and comfort him while I look at his wounds."

Timber locked his yellow eyes on Connor as Veronica and I slowly rolled him over to expose his belly. My initial reaction was the wounds inflicted by the mountain lion were severe and bleeding freely. Knowing I had to close the wounds before Timber bled out, I told Veronica, "In my saddlebags is another small leather bag with a tin of cranberry and charcoal poultice, a roll of catgut string, and several bone needles. Grab that, my long John underwear, and the bottle of drinking whiskey."

Veronica stood and moved with a sense of urgency while looking at Connor as she held Timber's eyes and kept him occupied. I thought how brave she was in keeping the white wolf calm; even if Timber succumbed to his wounds, he would go out of this world knowing the girl he saved loved him.

Before Veronica returned with my medical supplies and cranberry and charcoal poultice, I knew the almost full moon above was not enough to do what needed to be done. All the down firewood I could find went on top of the fire. I needed more light.

Veronica returned with everything I asked for plus two full canteens of water. As long as Connor comforted Timber with love, he was as docile as any house dog which amazed me to no end. I had no doubt that Timber believed we were trying to save his life. With his belly exposed and after cleaning the wounds with some fresh water and taping it with a cloth I had cut out of one leg of my long Johns, I determined that none of his vitals had been shredded. That was good news and hopefully would keep any infection from setting in after I closed the mountain lion slashes.

Looking at Veronica, I indicated with a nod of my head for her to look because I learned in the short time in knowing her to value her thoughts. After surveying the damage, she looked at me, "Not good, but could be a heck of a lot worse."

Cutting out another square of my long Johns, I placed the roll of cat gut and bone needles on top and poured the drinking whiskey over the thread and needles to sterilize them - something I had learned to do watching the surgeons work on the wounded during the Civil War. Having done that, I washed my hands with water and then poured a generous amount of whiskey on them as well in an attempt to clean them the best I could - considering the circumstances. Hoping Timber was in no mood to bite me or take my hand, I poured off about half the remaining whiskey into his open wounds. Dabbing the fingers of my right hand into the cranberry and charcoal poultice I spread it evenly into the wound just like I had seen the Ute Indian medicine men do.

Timber and Connor were still being champions, and both remained calm as they kept their eyes on one another. Threading the bone needle, I went to work and stitched all the five open wounds closed.

After feeling that I had doctored Timber to the best of my ability, the next step was to clean the outside of the wounds. After washing the battle wounds with water and whiskey, I dabbed them dry and surveyed my needlework. It would seem the bleeding had stopped. It was now time to apply more cranberry and charcoal poultice over the wounds in an effort to stave off any infection that could possibly lead to gangrene.

As I looked to the sky, the moon was directly overhead, and the air had gotten cold. Timber had collapsed far enough away from the fire that he could not feel the heat. Veronica and I tenderly moved timber onto a flannel blanket and then it took both of us with Connor's help to drag him closer to the fire. Veronica started making a bedroll for Timber while Connor and I gathered more wood for the fire.

Placing more wood on the fire increased the possibility of Alistair McPherson and the Highlander gang being able to locate us if he was closer than I believed. The smoke would be heavy in the air and carry farther than I would have liked. Looking at Connor's face and the love that had grown between her and the white wolf, I knew our priorities had changed. Trying to save Timber's life was now more important than getting to Alma. Timber had risked his life without hesitation to save Connor from the lion attack and I sure as hell would not put him down even if there was a remote chance of his pulling through this. If the time came and Timber had to be put down, it had to be Connor's decision and not mine. It was obvious that Timber belonged to her and her only.

Connor, with a flannel blanket pulled over her and the wolf, snuggled up to Timber. Connor's wolf was still struggling to breathe, but remained quiet. Thinking back, I had never heard a tale of a lone wolf killing a lion. Then again, I had never heard of a lion killing a lone wolf either. Wolves hunted in packs and I could only imagine that a lion would just turn the other way instead of taking on a pack of wolves. There was easier prey along the Rocky Mountain frontier that both lions and wolves did not need to prey on the other. If I had not seen it with my own eyes and just had heard the tale, I would not have believed it and thought the teller of the story was a liar.

With Connor and Timber settled in for the cold night and the fire at a full blaze, Veronica and I made ready our bedroll. We didn't even talk about it tonight; we gathered the makings of our bed together. Veronica and I - it would seem - were starting to anticipate each other's thoughts - it felt right to do so.

Now that our sleeping arrangements and bedroll had been established, I made sure my Colt and Winchester were fully loaded and laid the rifle within easy grasp. The handgun I would keep with me under the blanket. Veronica lay down facing the fire, and I lay down behind her, and without thinking I draped my left arm over her and pulled her in closer so I could keep her warm. Veronica laid her left hand on my hand and within a minute or two I could feel the rhythm of her sleep.

For up to thirty minutes after Veronica fell asleep, I listened to the night and the horses for anything out of the ordinary that would give the telltale sign that McPherson or his men were closing in. Hearing none and feeling we were safe for the remaining night, I finally fell asleep.

Chapter 22

When dawn broke, the morning sun brought the hint of a warmer day. Listening to the woods, I turned my head toward Gypsy and the other horses. All the horses were grazing peacefully showing no sense of an alarm. It would seem that for the time being we were safe from Alistair McPherson and his outlaws. I hoped that the Highlander had moved on to prey on much easier folks. Hopefully, we had proven ourselves to be too much of a pain in the butt. I didn't really believe that, but it was my hope.

I stood slowly as not to wake Veronica. It had been a long night for all of us with the mountain lion attack. Looking over to the spot where Connor was still sleeping cuddled up to her wolf, I feared that Timber had succumbed to his wounds during the evening and had expired. That would break my granddaughter's heart and not sure that was something I could deal with.

Any thought of Timber's passing was quickly dashed. As I bent down to check on Timber, the wolf opened his eyes and looked at me. I saw the determination of an animal that wanted to live. Unless his wounds got infected, it would seem that the white wolf was on the mend. As I pulled back the blanket, Timber let me gently roll him onto his back so I could look at his wounds. The stitches had not pulled away during the night even though the wounds had swelled some. It would seem that Connor had a calming effect on the wolf. Timber was not the petting type unless it happened to be Connor, but he let me stitch him up last night and was docile now as I inspected my handiwork.

Connor woke, and she looked at me first and then with all the love she could muster, she wrapped her arms around Timber's neck and pulled herself in with a devoted hug. Timber was like butter in her hands; last night he did the impossible and killed a mountain lion, but his wild and savage demeanor was put aside for a young girl. Connor smiled and her eyes caught mine. "Thank you grandpa, for saving Timber's life. And I know Timber is grateful."

Smiling back and feeling my love for the innocence of this girl who had my blood running through her veins, I spoke in a reassuring voice, "We will stay here long enough to let Timber heal up a tad and gain some of his strength back. In the meantime, we are going to have to take care of him instead of him taking care of us. What do you think of that, Connor?"

Connor sat up quickly and her eyes told me she was deep in thought. She replied after a few seconds, "That's a grand idea, grandpa."

Reaching out, I pet the side of Timber and spoke to Connor, "First things first, I need you to go grab the canteen of water and the tin of cranberry and charcoal poultice and bring them back. After that wake Veronica and get a fire going for some breakfast. Timber will need some bacon." Connor was quick about her new chore and brought the items I asked for. Then she returned to wake Veronica.

Pouring water into my cupped hand, I held it to Timber's awaiting mouth, and he greedily lapped up the water. He did not stop drinking until he had drunk the whole canteen of water. Once his thirst had been satisfied for now, I rolled him gingerly back over on his back and exposed his wounds and applied another coating of cranberry and charcoal poultice. Knowing Timber was a dandy and kept his snow white fur clean, I did what I could and picked the bigger chunks of mud and dried blood from his fur trying to freshen him up some. Timber, after he drank his fill of water, kept straining his neck keeping his eye on Connor as she moved about helping Veronica with the chore of getting breakfast ready. There was no doubt whatsoever in my mind that the yellow-eyed cur was a one person wolf.

Once the smell of bacon and beans were frying, I gave Timber one more pat on his head. It was my belief that Timber just needed time and that he would make a full recovery, which pleased my heart. I had become accustomed to having the wolf as part of my family.

As I passed Veronica as she was getting breakfast ready, our eyes met and she reached out and touched my hand as I continued on toward the horses. That one small touch was like I got hit by a lightning bolt. It startled me some and I tried not to show it, but Veronica caught it and she smiled that Veronica smile. With not one word, she had stirred my blood this morning. The thought of her leaving to return to home to her sister in Mexico ruined the moment and dimmed my mood. It would seem I was getting accustomed to having Veronica here, she had a way of making me remember the feelings that I had long thought dead. Not sure that was a good thing.

Gypsy, Spirit, and Outlaw were eager for the grain I gave them and a pinch of sugar for a treat. Knowing we were staying put for several days, I gave each of them a quick going over with my wooden curry comb. Grooming the horses, I thought about Alistair McPherson.

If the outlaw McPherson was the man I thought he was, there would be no backup in the Scottish renegade. My hope was that he decided to leave us be and let us go on with our lives, but I knew that would not be possible. I had killed his brother and between Ghost and me, we had wounded or killed six others in his gang. We may have lost them for now, and by staying here until Timber could travel would only anger the Highlander even more. My fear was that he would just bypass the hunt and head to Alma and would be there waiting for us to return. It would be what I would do. There was a chance by saving Connor and not killing Alistair in the process, that my daughter Jessica and her husband Brody had been put in harm's way. If Brody's father Finn was the man I thought he was, he would have beefed up his security after they had kidnapped Connor…or at least he should have. Pondering that last thought, now I was not so certain; other than that short spell of talking to Finn, I really did not know the man. All these thoughts bounced around in my thinker. Without knowing what lay ahead in Alma, I decided not to fret over what I could not change and pushed my worries to the back of my mind. Priorities had changed and for now the goal was to get the white wolf healthy enough to be on the trail again.

Breakfast was more about getting Timber fed than it was about Connor, Veronica, or myself. The white wolf, still lying on his side, downed a pound and a half of fat back bacon as Connor fed it to him by hand. Being hungry was a good sign of healing and could only help in getting his strength back.

Knowing we would be here for several days and that our supplies would run low, I dug out some of my jump traps and snares and made into the woods to catch us some fresh meat. I preferred not to use my rifle because the gunshot would only point those that were hunting us in the right direction. It had been longer than I would have liked before I had trapped my own food. As I began the task of setting out the traps, I thought how Ghost was the better mountain man and would have been more at home doing this. Thinking of Matt Lee sent a wave of guilt for leaving him there at the mouth of Phantom Canyon. Touching Ghost's letter to his wife in my pocket, I felt better knowing I would fulfill my promise to the legendary mountain man and return to Redemption Valley to bury the letter with Walk With Ghost.

Wild animals were just like most folks I know and were predictable in their routines, so I set my first jump trap on the well-worn path of a raccoon. Spending the rest of the morning, I located several game trails and set the rest of the snares and traps. For the next several days we - including Timber - ate fresh meat caught in my traps including raccoon, rabbit, and squirrel. Connor had not eaten squirrel before her kidnapping but did not squawk when it was offered on her dinner plate.

On the third day, Timber walked gingerly and seemed to be recovering nicely. On the fourth day the white wolf tagged along with Connor and me as we checked the snares and traps. Thinking it was Connor's decision, I asked her on the fourth night after the mountain lion's attack, "By my reckoning it is just over forty miles to Alma. Maybe three days on the trail. What do you think Connor, do you believe Timber is ready to travel?"

The fire was keeping the chill of the night at bay as Connor thought about my question. She looked at me and then at Timber before she replied in all seriousness, "Timber told me yesterday he was ready for the trail. I held off one more day because I was not sure, but after today I think he is ready."

Veronica's face lit up with a huge smile hearing Connor say Timber had talked to her. I almost laughed but thought better of it. Maybe the white wolf spoke to her in a manner that my granddaughter could only understand. Who was I to laugh at such a notion; I had seen stranger things along the Rocky Mountain frontier. Nodding my head "yes" I replied, "Then it is settled; at daybreak tomorrow we are heading to Alma."

Chapter 23

On the morning of the fifth day after the mountain lion attack, the sun appeared above the eastern horizon in all its orange and blue Rocky Mountain glory. The sky overhead was cloudless as I prepped Gypsy, Spirit, and Outlaw for the trail. And after a filling breakfast for all of rabbit and beans mopped up with campfire tortillas, we headed more north than west toward the town of Alma.

The weather during the last five days had been snowless and snow that had been on the south side of Current Creek Pass had melted leaving the trail north dry. Reaching the top of the pass, we were still within the evergreens and aspen trees since the pass was a good 1000 feet below timberline. The northern sky had darkened with storm clouds. Even though the storm that was brewing was in the distance in more miles than I care to count, it was something I needed to keep my eye on.

Slowing the pace in the beginning for Timber proved not to be needed; by mid-morning he was running ahead of me and looking back as if he was wondering what the hell was taking so long. It would seem that the white wolf was doing fine and almost mended from his wounds. After I gave Gypsy more rein and her head, Timber let me pass him and once again I took the point and the yellow-eyed wolf dropped back and took his normal position of rear guard just behind Connor.

At midday we stopped in the shadow of Three Mile Mountain to the east of us for a quick meal of venison jerky and leftover campfire tortillas. I wanted to check Timber's lacerations, and he let Connor and I roll him over on his back. The catgut stitch I had used to close the wounds had all but disappeared with no need to cut them loose. After I gave the tin of cranberry and charcoal poultice to Connor, she applied another coat of the healing Ute Indian concoction to the wolf's underbelly. After being doctored, Timber licked her hand, and Connor's face split with a smile and she hugged the neck of the enormous wolf. In her happy voice she said, "Isn't Timber the most loving wolf?"

Flashes of memory flooded my mind of the savage attacks that Timber had inflicted on Alistair McPherson's men and horses at the mouth of Phantom Canyon and the killing of the mountain lion. Knowing Timber was still a wild and savage beast when the need arose but as docile as a newborn pup with Connor, I replied, "Your grandpa doesn't know much Connor, but the one thing I do know is that Timber loves you more than he loves himself."

At midafternoon we stopped to water the horses and refill our canteens with some fresh creek water. Looking to the north at the clouds building over the horizon, I was deep in thought when Veronica rode up beside me and asked, "You seem troubled, Marshal. Is it that storm a brewing that has your thought?"

As I turned to look at Veronica, her deep dark brown eyes caught my attention more than they should have before I smiled and answered, "The storm has some of my thoughts, but I have been thinking more about what we might be facing once we reach Alma. My gut instinct is telling me that Alistair McPherson and his men have given up trying to trail us. If he had not, he would have caught up with us by now since we took the time for Timber to heal up."

Veronica looked confused. "That's a good thing-right?"

Shaking my head "no," I thought about if I should let Veronica know my true thoughts. Deciding it was her life in jeopardy as well as Connor's and my own, I told her, "A man like the Highlander became the outlaw he is because something is missing inside of him. Evil lives in all men, but a good man does not unleash it. I saw him when he killed Matt Lee, and there was no honor in his slaying. He did not respect the man who had fought his whole gang and wiped out half of it. Alistair McPherson has no goodness in him, and the evil controls him. He will not let it go that for one I took Connor from him; and for two I killed his brother. He stopped trailing us because he and his men are not skilled enough in woodcraft, but he is not stupid. McPherson knows where we are going and he probably is already there. My fear, Veronica, is not of any confrontation with this man or even losing my life. My fear is that my daughter Jessica and her husband Brody may be in jeopardy."

Veronica reached out and touched my cheek softly. "I have been taught from an early age, Eric, that for evil to prosper, good men do nothing. You are a good man, and you will do what needs to be done to protect your family or avenge them if needed. I have not known you for all that long but long enough to know you are a man to be reckoned with."

Giving Gypsy her head and some rein and a slight jab of my spur, I moved forward, but not without saying, "I am that Veronica. I have a skill set that some do not have."

By the time the sun dropped below the western horizon, we had moved onto the flat plateau of South Park. The dark clouds of the day stayed in the north but were closer and had the look of snow about them. The sky overhead though was clear with the stars abundant raining their light down upon us. It was a beautiful night.

With the horses taken care of - for what man would I be that did not see to his horses first - I took the supper plate offered by Connor. Leftover rabbit and beans with the last two cans of peaches from my supplies for dessert. With my plate cleaned, I set it aside when Connor came up and rolled into my lap like it was the place to be. Timber had followed her over and once Connor settled into my lap with her back toward my chest, the white wolf lay down on the ground at our feet and promptly fell asleep. I was thankful that Ghost and I had the gumption and the skill to take my granddaughter back from the Highlander. Just this moment of being with her as she looked to the heavens in wonder was worth all that it had cost to set her free. Connor, still looking upward above the campfire, said, "Grandpa the stars and the moon make me dream good dreams when I fall asleep looking at them."

Thinking how wonderful it would be to be young again, I sat with her for a full minute as we admired the same sky above. "You know my grandpa told me when I was about your age a secret. A secret I had to keep until I had a grandchild of my own to share it with. Do you want to know that secret?"

Connor spun her head so fast to look at me, and I could see the campfire's shimmering light in her eyes. Her smile spoke of childlike wonder and excitement. She reached out with her right hand and touched my cheek. "A secret? How wonderful is that? I want to know it."

All of Connor's attention was on me as if what I had to say was the most important thing in the world. "If I tell you the secret you have to promise that it will be only between you and me until you have your own grandchildren to tell it to. Do you promise?"

Connor knew this was an important thing, so she asked, "I can't tell mom or dad even?"

It would be difficult for such an angel to keep secrets from her parents. "It is okay to tell your parents, Connor, but only when they are sad and need to hear something good. Can you do that?"

Connor reached out now with her left hand and grabbed my face and whispered, "That is easy grandpa, and I can do that."

Taking my forefinger, I touched Connor's right ear. "My grandpa said if I listened closely to the silence of the night and if I tried real hard, I could hear the moon whisper. Grandpa told me the moon only talked and spoke its wisdom to those that wanted to hear it. He told me that the moon's whisper was nothing new. He spoke of how the old mountain men and Ute Indians of these Rocky Mountains had always been fascinated by the ancient moon down through the ages. Once I learned how to hear the whispers of the moon, it had a special meaning to me. Even as a small child, I was captivated by it; the moon and all its mystery spoke directly to me - or so I believed. It has always been my friend and ally when I had none. This romantic notion I have with the moon has never left me as I have grown older. Grandpa had even written a poem about it."

"The moon when I was little it would listen to me,
As I lay outdoors under the old evergreen tree.
Never judged me it always remained silent in the night,
Telling my secrets to the moon above only seemed right.
Blue or yellow the color of the moon didn't matter much,
The moon knew all my childhood fears, mysteries and such.
When I was young, I used to think the moon was only for me,
High in the heavens; on earth I was the only one it could see.
The moon above knew all my thoughts, hopes, and dreams,
All my expectations, visions, and imaginings rode those moon's beams.
When I was little, the moon was more than my friend high in the sky,
It helped me with my struggles and fears-it was my ally.
Sometimes, as I have gotten older, I lose touch with my moon,
When that happens, I look heavenward and get my life back in tune.
The moon when I was little it would listen to me,
As I lay outdoors under the old evergreen tree."

Connor's eyes were wide with wonderment and she cocked her ear to the sky to listen. Then a frown crossed her face when she said, "I don't hear it grandpa."

Touching her on the nose, "That's because you are just learning little one. I want you to close your eyes and focus on what you hear."

Connor did as I asked and she closed her eyes. I let her focus on the night for a few seconds, and then I said, "Without opening your eyes tell me what you hear."

Connor's face lit up with a smile. "I hear the wind in the evergreen trees as it whistles through the needles. There is an owl far off, but I hear its hoot." Opening her eyes, she said, "But others can hear those sounds as well Grandpa."

Smiling, I brought her in closer to my chest. "You see, that is where the secret comes in. Most people hear, but they ignore all that surrounds them so they really do not hear the wind whispers.

You now know without the moon and its whispers that there would be no melodies from the wind and the evergreens. That without the moon there would be no distant music from a faraway owl. The moon only whispers understanding to those that know the secret."

Connor's eyes filled with tears and understanding. The moon whispers had just opened a door to all the beauty that nature offered to my granddaughter. She held me tight in a hug and she told me what I needed to hear. "Oh, thank you grandpa, for telling me the secret. I love you for that!"

Chapter 24

The cold of the night woke me. Cuddled up next to Veronica, who was still sleeping, I looked toward the stars, but there weren't any. The storm I had watched all day in the north was now finally directly above and the temperature had fallen dramatically. Although it was not snowing yet, I could feel it in my bones and knew it would be snowing before daybreak. Just as I had that thought, a snowflake the size of my thumb landed on my face.

Gypsy, Spirit, and Outlaw could sense the storm and had moved close into what was left of the fire. I looked over to where Timber and Connor were sleeping; Timber was awake and looking toward the heavens as he sensed the storm.

As I stood, I tried not to disturb Veronica. By the time I had straightened out my knees and stood fully erect, the air was full of snowflakes carried on the northern wind. I opened my mouth and stuck out my tongue as I used to when I was just a boy so the snow could melt on it. The water of the virgin snow tasted sweet and clean with nature. The wind was picking up as the temperature continued to drop, reminding me of something I read from a long dead poet. "To appreciate the beauty of a snowflake, it is necessary to stand out in the cold." I could not remember the name of the poet, but his words were never truer.

Thinking about the day ahead and whether this storm turned into an early winter blizzard, I thought that it would not behoove us for it to catch us on the high mountain plateau of South Park. There was no shelter from the wind, for the trees were far away on the mountains that surrounded us. Looking about this choice I had picked for a campsite, I thought that there was actually no better place on the high mountain plains of South Park to sit out a northern blow. We had camped on the south side of a knoll that would cause it to lift any drifting snow up and over us to be deposited even further south. I planned ahead as I kept tabs on the storm; Connor, Veronica, and I had gathered any wood that had been scattered on the trail and any dried cow pies we could find. This northerner may turn out to be a flash in the pan, but it was best to just stay here and wait out the storm just in case.

Dawn broke across the eastern horizon, and the new grayish light of the new day showed a dreary and thankless sky above and the promise of more for the day. It was a good day to stay put and ride out the storm.

As I was looking to the horses to get them ready for the incoming storm, Veronica and Connor woke and started the chore of stirring the fire into a workable warming and cook fire. Veronica asked while I was giving each of the horses some grain from my dwindling supply, "Will the horses scatter if the storm gets any worse?"

Rubbing Gypsy's ear the way she liked it, I replied to Veronica, "Since we are south of the knoll which will prevent any drifting of snow to pile up here, the horses will stay close. They will instinctively know this is the best place to be out of the wind. They will not wander away as long as we are here."

Veronica reached out and touched my hand in an almost loving manner, and our eyes caught for a second and I liked what I saw there. I would miss this woman when we got to Alma and she catches the stage back to Mexico. It darkened my heart to think of it, so I pushed that thought to the back of my mind.

By the time I finished with the horses, the wind was gusting so hard that at the time it sounded just like a freight train. The snow had gotten heavy and the sky above and all around us had turned into a whiteout, and I was thankful we had the knoll to keep the northern beast of a storm at bay.

The horses, as I knew they would, stayed close and out of the wind with us on the southern side of the knoll. Connor, Veronica, Timber, and I huddled near the fire as we ate our breakfast of roasted squirrel and fried beans. Timber ate along with us like a normal house dog just so long as it was Connor that fed him. It still amazed me how Connor had been able to almost tame the wild and savage side of the yellow-eyed wolf.

With breakfast and the morning chores completed, all that was left for us to do was to hunker down and stay warm. We laid out our blankets in such a manner as that we all could share the warmth of each other. Veronica was on my right; Connor was curled up in my left arm with Timber to the left of Connor. Timber, being accustomed to the cold winter, knew it was best just to catch some shut-eye now and wait out the storm. He promptly fell asleep and his snoring brought giggles from Connor.

Connor looked up into my eyes and said, "If it was not for you being here grandpa, I would be scared."

Looking my granddaughter in her eye I replied, "Fear is nothing but a dose of a healthy respect for events you cannot change or have any control of. A blizzard, thunder, lightning, and tornadoes are the Lord's ways of showing us it is he that is really in control of our destiny. In his wisdom, though with adverse weather, he has woven all the aspect of the beauty of nature for all to see. Once you realize this, you can set the fear aside and enjoy the beauty of his creations. Look above us Connor, and watch the snow swirl and then watch it head south to drift beyond our campsite. Watch and focus on the snow and you will see the crystals glint as they reflect the campfire."

Connor, with the wondering of a child, looked straight up and within seconds her smile spread across her face. "I see it grandpa, I see it!"

Smiling to myself remembering my youth when looking at my granddaughter, I said, "As we hunker down, we will ponder if the blizzard will last forever, but when it's done we will realize it didn't last as long as we thought. Once the storm is finished, we will look across the snowdrifts and consider the meaning of life in the cold and the silence. This is a good thing and we must cherish those moments in life, just like the moon whispers; it is only for those that take the time to look and listen. When you come out of a storm such as this, you are never the same person when it first started. You have taken the time to learn about yourself and the more you know about yourself, the better off you are. But Connor, the best is yet to come. There is nothing more powerful than that feeling of walking across the unbroken snow, knowing it has never been walked on before."

Connor followed Timber into slumber land, and then Veronica fell asleep. With my new tribe all asleep but me, I thought about Alma and what I was sure awaited us there. Alistair McPherson and what remained of the Highlander gang would be in town by now. After kidnapping Connor, the Highlander gang would be known men there and could not simply wait it out until we got there. McPherson would be a man used to getting his way and if anyone stood in front of his mission, he would kill that person. My thought is that he and his gang could probably not hide in plain sight in town. He might have taken the town by storm and has taken the whole place hostage including my daughter Jessica and her husband Brody. It was my hope the other grandpa Finn O'Brien would have enough hired guns to keep our family and the town safe. I did not know Finn all that well and I could not count on that, and I knew that I would have to play as if I was a lone man on a mission. Touching my vest pocket, I could feel the letter that Matt Lee had written his wife before his death and I wished the legendary mountain man was still by my side. I had gotten used to having the Ghost's wisdom of the Rocky Mountains and his superior fighting skills protecting my back. If I should die once reaching Alma, then Matt Lee's death would have been for nothing and I could not have that. Where there is a will, there is a way my daddy used to say. I would just have to play it by ear and gut instinct and hope the Lord knew I was on the righteous side.

With the storm still raging above and with nothing more to ponder, I knew it was time for sleep. Below the swirling storm, the warmth of my loved ones made me feel sleepy. Before falling asleep, I bolted awake and the thought of including Veronica in my last thought as a loved one startled me. I had thought it as if it was the right thing to think without hesitation. It felt right and natural. Shaking my head, I whispered to myself, "I will be damned, I think I have fallen in love with the widow from Mexico!"

Chapter 25

The blizzard we were experiencing as far as blizzards go was not all that bad but just bad enough to keep us all squatted down and out of the wind. The snow amount was just enough to make the sky a white-out, but accumulations were not too much. By midday the swirling snow that was being lifted over the knoll had only made a drift about a foot and a half tall just twenty yards south of our campsite. The temperature out of the gusting wind was just a tad below freezing, which just made it somewhat uncomfortable away from the fire. There was not much to do but cuddle up next to the fire and wait out the storm. With all the sleep we were getting as we waited, all of us would be well rested once we resumed the trail.

At mid-afternoon I moved to the top of the knoll for a look see to the north, and the wind had dwindled as the storm started to lose its punch. Looking straight up into the whiteness over my head, I could see the hint of blue sky above the churning snow telling me the storm was just about over. I reckoned by morning we would be able to move out and be back on the trail.

At sundown the storm had moved south, leaving the sky cloudless, and we could see the full grandeur of a Rocky Mountain sunset on the western horizon. The cold air brought out the blue and orange that shimmered above the distant snow-capped mountains reminding me once again what a wonderful and glorious place to spend my life. I could think of no other place I would rather be. Because what snow there was had drifted over us, there was none at all on the ground around our camp. On the trail tomorrow there would be snow drifts but easily avoidable because of the lack of overall snow in the storm.

The sunset turned into a night full of twinkling stars and a glowing moon as Connor, Veronica, and I listened to the moon whispers. Connor, after asking me if it was okay, told Veronica the secret of the moon whispers, telling the tale and the secret as if she had been saying it for years. We all would listen to the night and then add something we had heard so the others could focus in on it. The moon whispers were turning out to be a grand learning experience for Connor in the ways of the wilderness. I loved every minute.

The next morning we all were well rested and eager for the trail. Gypsy, Spirit, and Outlaw were even tossing their heads and stomping their hooves in anticipation of moving out. In just one day we all had a bit of cabin fever. The trail northwest to Alma seemed to be calling us.

The air this morning was crisp and cool, and the snow drifts from the northern storm were few and far between and did not slow us down as we easily zigged and zagged in between them. By mid-afternoon we reached the southern end of the town of Hartsel. Seeing the town brought a flash of memory; not that long ago Matt Lee and I had ridden through this town on the way to Phantom Canyon to rescue Connor. I touched Ghost's letter in my vest to make sure I still had it. Feeling relieved, I had not lost the mountain man's letter to his wife; it would bother me to no end if I could not fulfill my promise to the legendary mountain man.

We were short of supplies due to the delay of letting Timber heal up after he tangled with the mountain lion and the small blizzard we encountered, so I reined Gypsy in the direction of the dry goods store to stock up. The store keep was a man about forty years old with a bald head and walrus mustache. His arms were well muscled from moving heavy sacks and crates of merchandise. His name was Patrick with no last name given and seemed a friendly sort of a fellow. After he started to fill my order, I asked him, "Have there been several men traveling hard heading north in the last seven to eight days?"

Patrick stopped and looked at me determining if he should talk to me. He kind of shrugged his shoulders as if he decided it really didn't matter if he told me or not. So he answered my question, "Yes, a week ago today. They stopped and paid cash for 500 44 caliber cartridges. The leader with a funny accent told him that they had business to take care of in Alma. They had the look of hard men, and I did not question them on what type of business. The one thing I know mister, with that kind of ammo, their business was of the killing kind."

The leader with the "funny accent" had to be Alistair McPherson, who probably spoke with a Scottish accent. The one thing Patrick had confirmed was that McPherson had lost us on the trail and once he realized that, he made a beeline to Alma. If he passed through here seven days ago, it meant he had been in Alma for the last five days. Hard to say what havoc the remaining Highlander gang had caused on the good folks in Alma. My gut instinct told me my daughter and son-in-law were in trouble. I tried to clear my thoughts, for worrying now would get me nowhere, but lost sleep. We were still a good day and a half away southeast of Alma and distressing about it would not make it any better. Waving Patrick the store keep over, "I need to add fifty 44 caliber cartridges and two boxes of 12 gauge double ought buck to my order."

Patrick without hesitation responded, "Will do. It seems everyone is stocking up on ammo these days. Sort of reminds me what my Pappy used to say, 'Guns don't kill people; the killing part is the one pulling the trigger.'" It would seem that Patrick's Pappy was a man of my own thinking.

After loading the supplies, I reined Gypsy north and gave her a small jab of my spur and in no time we were back on the trail toward Alma. The mood of Veronica and Connor had gotten somber since they both had overheard Patrick when he told of the men heading north. They both knew this ordeal with the Highlander Gang was far from being over.

About an hour before the sun dropped below the western horizon, we were about a mile short of Garo and made camp outside of the town. I was not in the mood to be talking to strangers tonight. From this point on, I had to treat the trail ahead as hostile territory.

After I had seen to the horses, Veronica and Connor had prepared a quick supper of chicken eggs and fat backed bacon we had gotten in Hartsel. Veronica knew my mind was occupied with what lay ahead and she kept Connor busy with talk about her mom and dad and home.

I, on the other hand, had chores to do this evening that involved getting ready to finish up what Ghost and I had started at the mouth of Phantom Canyon. I sharpened my Bowie knife and made sure my cartridge loops were full of 44 cartridges. After cleaning my Colt pistol, I spun the cylinder to the chamber normally kept empty for safety and loaded it with a 44 cartridge. Having completed that, I turned my attention to cleaning my lever action Winchester and the 12 gauge Greener shotgun. I had not needed the shotgun in the battle at Phantom Canyon, but I had a feeling it would come in handy in Alma. For this to be over, I would have to kill Alistair McPherson and his men. McPherson would not forgive and forget that Ghost and I had bested them at Phantom Canyon and that I had killed his brother. There was no doubt that blood was going to be shed in Alma. The question was whose blood was it going to be - mine or the Highlander Gang's?

Thinking ahead, I knew we had at least one more day on the trail before reaching Alma. During the next twenty-four hours, I had to decide how to keep Connor and Veronica safe before I entered the gold mining town to hunt down the men that were hunting us.

Connor and Timber had cuddled up for the night and were fast asleep. Veronica and I stayed awake a little longer watching the fire in silence when I told her what was on my mind. "Veronica, when we get to Alma, I am going to have to kill Alistair McPherson and his men. I see no other avenue that keeps us all safe."

Veronica stood and walked over and opened my blanket and moved inside of it to be next to me. Her nearness set my blood on fire and made my fingers tingle. She then laid her head on my shoulder before speaking, "Eric Robert, with all the men I have known in my life, I have never met such a man as you. Your relationship with your granddaughter shows you are a loving, caring, and thoughtful man. The other side of that is you can be ruthless and deadly when the need and events call for it. I know you have to end this, and Alistair McPherson has left you no choice. No matter what Eric Robert, you need to focus on what needs to be done. I realize it, and I believe Connor knows that there will be bloodshed and you will be the one that has to do it. We both know if you could have avoided it, you would have, but they forced this confrontation. If you are worried about what we would think of you when this is done - quit it."

Veronica seemed to understand me better than myself. I worried what she and Connor may think of me after slaying the outlaws that were waiting in ambush for us. It eased my mind that she knew it had to be done. As I held her tight and felt her warmth and giving her mine, it was not long before we both fell asleep.

Chapter 26

Waking an hour before dawn, I stirred the remnants of last night's fire into a small flame and then added some kindling. Once the fire took hold, I added more wood until there was a sizeable cooking fire.

I looked above into the fading night sky, and it was cloudless with only the North Star, the brightest of all the stars, remaining. I watched the star as its brightness diminished as the day took hold just like yesterday and every day before down through the history of the world. It makes a man such as I realize how trivial our lives were compared to that of these white shrouded mountains of old. No matter what happens today or tomorrow on the streets of Alma, Colorado, time will go on with me either standing upright or lying six feet below ground. Yes, the Rocky Mountains, the stars above, the wind, the evergreen, and aspen trees in their own majestic way humbled us all. It all sort of boggled my mind pondering on it. One thing I knew is if death awaited me in the next twenty-four to forty-eight hours, I was taking that Scottish renegade Alistair

McPherson and his kind with me. If there was to be a place in hell waiting for me for all things I had done or was about to do, then McPherson would be right alongside me knowing for eternity he messed with the wrong family.

The air this early morning was crisp but not too cold, and the wind had faded just like the North Star into the night. Warming my hands over the fire, I watched over those I cared for the most. Connor was still sleeping, but Timber was wide awake watching me as he stayed still as not to disturb my granddaughter cuddled up to his back keeping warm. Veronica was soundlessly sleeping and as I watched her for a spell, I realized again how I had fallen in love with this woman. Falling in love had been the furthest thing from my mind when I started this quest to rescue Connor. Life was always putting obstacles in my path or maybe it was an opportunity to settle my heart. I would have to ponder on it some to decide which it was.

I cleared my mind of family and love, for it would do me no good to have such thoughts when facing McPherson and what remained of the Highlander gang. I needed my heart to be cold and black; I needed my killer instinct to take over. Having a killer instinct is very spiritual; the power of ending a man's life and taking everything he ever was or will ever be away from him is akin to godlike. This was nothing I sought or wanted to do, but it is the will to survive and protect those whom I care for and love that gave me the black heart needed to do what had to be done. Alistair McPherson would know the moment I rode into Alma that hell and the specter of death rode alongside of me.

Thinking about the trail ahead and the last sixteen miles that would bring us to Alma, I figured it would take the better part of the day to get there and we should ride into town just as darkness fell. I would have to decide if the night was the best time to confront my enemies or to do so in the morning hours. I would have to think about that for a spell.

Veronica and Connor had woken up, and they started the chore of getting breakfast going, and I took my normal chore of getting Gypsy, Spirit, and Outlaw ready for the trail. Timber the white wolf, as was his routine, stayed close to Connor. As I used the wooden curry comb on Gypsy, my thoughts wandered back to the legendary mountain man Matt Lee. I felt his presence this morning as if he was almost in camp with me and was just standing behind my shoulder. It was a peaceful feeling and not a bad feeling of suspense or uneasiness. I had been brought up in the church and believed in the Lord Almighty, but not sure if I had ever thought about ghost if there was such a thing. Matt Lee was here this morning and just that feeling of him looking over my shoulder felt right. Maybe I was losing my mind; maybe I wasn't, but I felt his spirit here with me.

Shortly after breakfast and with the trail toward Alma beckoning, we left the comfort of our camp for the uncertainty of what lay ahead. The trail was flat with little or no snow on it and the drifts were few and far between. At noon we made the town of Fairplay. This mining camp was settled during the Pikes Peak gold rush and was by far the biggest settlement in the South Park region. Fairplay was just east of the middle fork of the South Platte River. Alma was northwest of Fairplay and just beyond that was Hoosier pass. With no need to stop, we just skirted the edge of town and kept moving northwest toward Alma.

At midafternoon still riding the banks of the middle fork of the South Platte River and just two miles south of Alma, I pulled up on Gypsy's reins and brought her to a standstill. After running some thoughts through my mind, I reined Gypsy around, riding back to be side by side of Veronica and Connor. Timber took my place in the front as soon as I vacated it as if by instinct he knew to keep track and be on guard for anything that might be out of kilter.

Clearing my voice, I spoke to my granddaughter, "Connor I need your help. I am not familiar with any folks in Alma and know of no one I can trust. I believe that the men that kidnapped you will already be in town and waiting for us. This ordeal will not be over until I have a final showdown with Alistair McPherson and his men. The problem is for me to do so I will need to hunt these men down. As much as I would hate for it to happen, it could turn into a running gun battle in the center of town. I can't be worried about protecting Veronica and you while I do this. I need a place to hide the both of you until this is all over. Do you have any ideas?"

Connor's eyes clouded as she gave my questions some thought and then they brightened up and she said, "We could probably stay at the Frey's. Heidi is my teacher, and she was there the day I was kidnapped. Her husband Ray is the blacksmith in town. They live in a little wooden house on a road named Chisholm Way, and we will just ride past it before we get into town."

Running this new information through my brain pan, I decided it was the best-case scenario and as I reined Gypsy back to the front I said, "That's the plan then. If the Frey's will have you, then I will leave you both there with them."

Less than an hour later, we approached the little wooden house on the banks of the middle fork of the South Platte River. The well taken care of house was made from wood planks and not the lodge pole pine logs you would expect to see in a mountain mining camp. The house and the small barn that sat next to it were painted a dark red as was the custom of such buildings. Ranchers, miners, folks from towns, and farmers would seal their wood plank barns and houses with linseed oil. To this oil, they would add a variety of things, most often it would be rust. Rust was plentiful here in these mining towns. The added rust turned the linseed oil red and it would help seal the wood better and kill any of the mountain mosses that might grow on buildings.

A middle-aged, grey-haired woman whom I assumed was Connor's teacher named Heidi, opened the door, and her eyes welled up with tears as soon as she saw Connor standing there. Connor broke down and cried and both gathered each other in their arms. A well-muscled, middle-aged man with a bald head and a heavy unkempt mustache whom I took to be Ray, Heidi's husband the blacksmith, stood back and was all smiles as he gazed upon my granddaughter. This reaction was well worth everything that had happened since the battle at Phantom Canyon. These good folks obviously loved my granddaughter, and I felt it was the right decision to leave her here before confronting what was left of the Highlander gang.

At first the Frey's were wary of the yellow-eyed wolf, but that quickly was dismissed as they saw how loyal Timber was to Connor and stayed by her side.

The Frey's invited all of us including Timber in, and the overpowering smell of fresh bread made my stomach rumble. Heidi didn't even ask if we were hungry; she just ushered us to the rough-hewn wood table and went about setting up plates of fresh bread and bowls of venison stew in front of us. Timber even got his own bowl of stew and bread but served on the floor. The home-cooked food was much appreciated by Connor, Veronica, and myself after having lived out of our saddlebags and off the land for such a long duration.

During supper proper introductions were made and then the Frey's spent upwards of an hour explaining of some mysterious men that had ridden into town over a week ago and had seemed to have taken up residence at the O'Brien Mining Company. That these hard looking and dangerous men would take turns going across the road to the Alma Saloon for food and drink. Three times a day they would cart food back to the mining company presumably for Finn, Brody, and my daughter Jessica. The O'Brien's went about doing business as usual but always had at least one of the mystery men with them at all times. There was plenty of talk about the mining settlement on what these mystery men were up to, but since it had appeared that no one was being held hostage or any of the town's laws had been broken, there was nothing that anyone could do other than to speculate on their intentions.

I explained to the Frey's that these men were in fact Alistair McPherson and the Highlander Gang that had kidnapped Connor. It confused me why no one recognized them as the outlaws they were until Ray explained there was only one man who had come to the Alma school to kidnap Connor and the one who had taken Connor was not among those at the O'Brien Mining Company. Connor quickly added that was because the one who had kidnapped her was Alistair's brother Alban, whom I had shot and killed during the Phantom Canyon battle.

As the sun slowly dropped below the western horizon, I thought long and hard about what my next step was. Veronica and Connor, as long as they stayed put here with the Frey's, would be safe. Ray Frey seemed to be a no nonsense man and in just the short time I had gotten to know him, I knew he would do what he had to do to keep the dark-eyed beauty Veronica and Connor safe. I had no qualms leaving them here in care of Ray and Heidi Frey.

It would seem that Alistair McPherson and the Highlander Gang were concentrated in two places in town - the Alma Saloon and the O'Brien Mining Company. That narrowed it down some for me. I was starting to think it was best to confront them in the dark, and tonight was just as good as any other night. The darkness would give me the ability to ride into town without being observed. My hope was they would expect a man, a woman, and Connor; not a lone rider. It was a stretch, but it may buy me valuable minutes to get in close.

Having decided to force the confrontation with McPherson tonight, I knew the hardest part was yet to come - not facing four armed men that meant me harm, but of having to say goodbye to Veronica and Connor possibly for the last time.

Chapter 27

Under the darkness and the shining stars above as I was putting my Winchester and Greener shotgun into their scabbards that rode on opposite sides of Gypsy's saddle, Connor and Veronica came to me reluctantly. As I turned my body toward Veronica, my eyes landed on her dark, bright fire lit eyes and I could see the hint of a tear forming.

Feeling Connor grab my hand gently, I lowered myself to look her straight on. For several seconds neither of us spoke as we looked at each other and then Connor's upper lip trembled slightly. Reaching out, I gently touched her lip with my forefinger and spoke quietly to my granddaughter, "Be strong little one, because I am going to be."

Connor leaned closer to me with her eyes never wavering from mine and with a slight quiver in her voice spoke, "I am so scared grandpa that I am going to lose you. I don't want you to go!"

Reaching out, I pulled Connor into my arms and held her tight like only a grandpa could do. "Connor, I don't want to go, but go I must. These men, these bad men will not give up, and it has fallen on me to make them see the wrong in what they have done. I have to go and I have to go bravely, for justice must be done and there must be accountability. I will not lie to you, Connor; there is a high possibility I will not come back. I guess in this life that is just part of loving someone; sometimes you have to give them up. I know this is tough on both of us, but these last few days we got to spend more quality time with each other than most grandpas and granddaughters get to do in a lifetime. We need to cherish that and keep those memories alive. Do you think you can do that for me?"

Connor tilted her head down, but her eyes still held mine as if she was trying to look over the tears, "Yes, grandpa I can do that."

Letting her go, I slowly extended her backwards as I looked upon this youngster that had stolen my heart these last several days. Smiling at my granddaughter at that moment was the toughest thing I had ever had to do, but smile I did. Keeping my voice calm was difficult as I spoke, "You need to go over there with Heidi and Ray while I talk to Veronica for a minute."

Connor hesitantly moved away toward Heidi and her husband Ray. About halfway Connor quickly spun back to look at me and spoke from her heart, "I love you grandpa!"

Now standing and still looking at my granddaughter, "I know you do Connor; just know you are the most important thing in my life and I love you to the moon and back!"

Connor finally broke and could not hold back the flood of tears as she turned and ran past the Frey's into their house. She was doing her best to be brave. I loved her for that.

Now turning my full attention to Veronica, I could see her upper lip trembled slightly before she regained her composure as any strong and independent woman would. The widow from Mexico was trying not to show her concern, but failing at it. Veronica spoke first, "Eric, I just want to thank you for all that you have done for me – the rescue, your kindness, the feeling of being safe with you. I refuse to say goodbye because goodbye means going away and going away means forgetting. I never will forget you Eric…never!"

Veronica had stood apart from me, not sure of the distance and what our relationship had become or at least not wanting to admit how we had grown to care for each other. Well, I would be damned if I rode away without telling this woman how I felt. Clearing my voice, "Well Veronica, I will not ride away and get shot all to pieces without telling you how I feel. Not much of a wordsmith nor a lady's man, so please forgive me as I stumble along here. The saddest part of tonight is having to say goodbye to someone I want to spend the rest of my life with. I tell you Miss Flores, saying goodbye to the woman I have fallen in love with is not easy. Just know if I survive this encounter with Alistair McPherson and his men, I am riding back here with every intention of making you my wife."

With having said more than I should, I pulled Veronica into my arms before she could say anything, and I kissed her like she needed to be kissed. She didn't quiver; she didn't try to pull back, and I took this to be a good sign. Stepping back from our kiss, I could see in her eyes she was already my woman, and it felt damn good. Veronica, as I knew she would, found her strength and with no more tears she said what I needed to hear, "I love you Eric Robert; now go do what needs to be done and get your butt back here as fast as Gypsy can carry you!"

Stepping into the stirrup, I got myself squared away in the saddle as I watched Veronica, Heidi, and Ray Frey as they all followed Connor into the little wood plank house. The only ones left were Gypsy, Timber the yellow-eyed wolf, and myself. As I studied Timber, it surprised me he had not followed Connor inside. Pointing toward the house, I spoke to the white wolf, "You best get inside and keep an eye on our girl."

Timber sat there staring at me. Thinking he wasn't going anywhere far, I let him be, and I reined Gypsy toward Alma and the destiny that awaited me there. Just as I was going to give Gypsy a slight jab of my spur, Timber took the point in front of us. Pulling back on the reins, I brought Gypsy to a halt and looked at Timber. "Where exactly are you, mutt? You need to stay here."

Timber sat on his hunches and just returned my stare. Rolling it around some in my brain pan, I decided that Timber was his own man and if he thought it was the best way to protect Connor was by going with me, I sure as hell could not change his mind. Maybe the white wolf was the advantage I needed to come out of this alive. Giving Gypsy some rein and her head, we took the trail toward Alma. Timber took point once again.

As I rode toward Alma, there was a cool northern breeze that spoke of the winter storms to come. It had a chill that shivered me some, so I turned my collar of my coat up to help some to keep me warm. The sky was empty, but that of a full moon and a few of the brightest stars that shone through the moon's brightness.

As I drew closer to my destination, my mood changed from that of a caring man into that of a man that could not care. For what was to come, I needed to reach down for that killer instinct and black heart that lived within me. It would not be to my benefit if I worried about my death; for once a man worries about his own demise, he does foolhardy things that actually get him killed. There was no turning back, I would either survive or die - it was that simple.

Bringing Gypsy to a halt just on the southern edge of Alma, I could hear the melody of an out of tune piano as it wafted down the main street of town. Timber moved silently to the right side of me as he surveyed the town as did I. We both listened to the night and by the light of the moon, we could see a few of the townsfolk as they moved along the boardwalk. A few, but not many, of the broad glass windows of the houses, were lit up with the dancing firelight of kerosene lamps. The town of Alma looked peaceful. Before tonight would be over, the specter of death would come to Alma. It was yet to be determined whose life would be extinguished - theirs or mine. Unafraid of losing my life, I spoke to the white wolf, "Timber, are you ready to go have a 'come to Jesus' moment meeting with some Scottish gentlemen?"

Timber stood without looking at me with his nose pointed northward. I took that as a "yes" and pulled my Greener 12-gauge double-barrel shotgun from its scabbard and checked the loads. Laying the greener crossways just behind the horn of my saddle, I gave Gypsy her head, and we moved forward…slowly.

Passing the first house on the southern end of town, I could smell the burning of tobacco before I could see two men in the shadows of a porch awning as they enjoyed their evening pipes before going to bed. Each puff on their pipes brought forth a glowing red-orange hue that lit their faces just for a second. These were not the men I sought. As we rode past the pipe-smoking men, I could feel their eyes watching Timber and me, and I heard one of them speaking to the other, "That looks like a damn wolf with that fellow."

Kurt James

Chapter 28

All my senses were heightened and on alert. My eyes were keen tonight and seemed to penetrate the darkness better than usual. It was almost as if I could hear beyond the walls and doors of the houses and business as we slowly made our way down the main street of Alma. Every smell of this mining camp seemed present; I could smell hay, dust, sweat, stale whiskey, and even the stinging aroma of the outhouses dotted throughout the town. Timber could sense the tension that flowed from my body, and he was also in tune with all that surrounded us.

Several minutes passed before Gypsy brought us to the boardwalk in front of the Alma Saloon. I could hear laughter and the music of "I'll Take You Home Again, Kathleen" as someone played it on the out-of-tuned piano. As I looked across the roadway to the front doors of the O'Brien Mining Company, not one light shone through the windows. I wondered if someone, hidden in the darkness beyond the windows, was watching me.

Once out of the saddle and with my boots firmly on the ground, I didn't tie off Gypsy's reins at the hitching post, I wanted her to be able to scatter once the shooting started. I pulled her nose close so I could nuzzle with my cheek. After a few seconds of loving Gypsy, I spoke softly so only she could hear, "Gypsy Girl once you hear gunshots and if it all goes south and I don't make it out of this saloon alive, you hightail it back to Veronica and Connor." Gypsy nodded her head twice and leaned into me a little closer as if she understood. What a wonderful horse and companion she had been.

Timber had already traversed the steps to the boardwalk and stood on top of the wood planking looking at me as if wondering what was taking me so long. Leaving my Winchester in the scabbard on my saddle, I carried the Greener shotgun in my left hand leaving my right gun hand free. Once I found myself standing side by side next to Timber, I touched my shirt pocket that carried Matt Lee's letter to his wife as if it would give me the extra edge I needed to survive what was about to come. Looking at Timber as he stood ready by my side, I said, "Time to settle this Timber for once and for all; let's send some Scottish outlaws back home to their maker!"

Using the tip of the shotgun, I pushed on the right side of the batwing door and entered the Alma Saloon. Timber had to duck underneath the left batwing door as he made his presence known.

The piano player stopped, and each man in the room turned to look at the newcomers - first me and then their eyes landed on the yellow-eyed white wolf. All were trying to gauge in their minds if we were a threat. There were seven men in the saloon not counting the barkeep and the piano player. None of the seven possible combatants were Alistair McPherson. None of the others looked familiar, but I didn't expect them to. The fight at Phantom Canyon was fast and furious and after killing the Highlanders brother Alban and the other one guarding Connor and Veronica, the only one of the remaining outlaws I got a good look at was Alistair himself. Any of the seven men in the saloon could be the other three remaining outlaws or none of them could be. I was just going to deal this out and see where the cards landed. All of the men, with their curiosity satisfied for the moment, returned to doing what they had been doing prior to us entering the saloon.

Moving to the end of the bar, I stayed to the far right, which left everyone in the Alma Saloon to my left. This way I could see and keep track of every man in the saloon and the front entrance.

Timber followed me and instinctively stayed to my left in between me and everyone else. Timber's hackles on his back and neck stood straight up as he kept a watchful eye on four men at one table. It was possible that the wolf could smell or recognize those that had been fighting against himself and Matt Lee. Once reaching the bar, I laid the Greener on top with the barrels pointed to my left and motioned the older, thinning grey haired barkeep over. Reaching into my vest pocket, I produced a five dollar gold piece and tossed it on the bar where it landed with a heavy clatter. Looking the barkeep in the eye and keeping my voice low, "A shot of whiskey and some information. I am Marshal Eric Robert, and I am looking for some men. These men would have been new in town and would have been here less than ten days. Do any of these men in here tonight fit that description?"

The bartender wiped down the bar in front of me with a filthy rag and without looking up at me or at the other men in the saloon, he spoke only loud enough that I could hear him, "I know who you are, Marshal. The three gents playing cribbage at the table are local gold miners and have been here several years. The other four sitting at the other table playing 5-card stud have been here in town for the last week or so. They drink their whisky and eat here and move back and forth across to the O'Brien Mining Company several times a day. Everyone in town is curious who they are. They seem to be waiting for something or maybe someone."

Turning slowly as to not to attract attention, I looked at the four men playing 5-card stud. Timber kept looking at these gentlemen with his hair on edge and ignored the other three playing cribbage. That was enough for me to know I was looking at some remaining Highlander gang members. I was confused about what the barkeep had said about them all being newcomers. Only four survived the battle of Phantom Canyon and one of those was the outlaw boss Alistair McPherson. None of the well-heeled gentlemen at that table was the Scottish Highlander.

Thinking this new information over and running it through my brain pan a couple of times, I thought it was highly possible that in the days following the battle of Phantom Canyon that McPherson had recruited some new members for his gang. That was a sobering thought for if that was true and now it seemed to be, I had no idea how many men were stacked up against me. The number of men here in the Alma Saloon or over at the O'Brien Mining Company was now not a known figure. One thing I know to be true is when your family and loved ones' very futures are at stake, then the odds against you don't matter. You just pull up your pants, tighten your belt buckle and move forward.

One of the men from the 5-card stud table kept glancing my way as if he was trying to figure out if he had seen me before. It surprised me that Timber's presence didn't give it all away, but then again, they never saw Timber with the one that had rescued Connor and Veronica. Timber hightailed it out of there in a different direction once they killed Matt Lee. My not getting a good look at those outlaws that were battling Matt Lee during the melee would also be true for them not getting a good look at me as well. I could see this dark-haired outlaw shifting back and forth between the white wolf and me, and then the moment of clarity crossed over his face and his eyes landed on mine. The time of the reckoning for kidnapping Connor and killing Matt Lee was fast approaching.

The dark-haired gunman stood slowly and I now could see he wore two Colts with their grip handles forward. Men who wore their weapons such as this fancied themselves fast on the draw. As he stood, so did Timber, and the white wolf crouched as if ready to attack. I slowly moved the Greener shotgun until I pointed it in the direction of the 5-card stud table.

The other three that had been seated at the green felted poker table also turned, and it finally dawned on them that the one they were waiting for was now in the room with them. They all in one motion stood as well to face Timber and myself. The remaining three were armed with one Colt each and riding their right hips. All looked at the Greener shotgun pointed in their direction and to the man they knew that no matter what happened in the next ticks of time that some or maybe all of them would not make it out of the Alma Saloon alive.

The men playing cribbage saw and felt the tension in the room, and they stood and silently moved toward the bat-wing doors and made their exit. I could sense the barkeep behind me as he and the piano player also made their exit through a door in the back of the saloon. Timber and I now stood alone facing the four remaining men. This confrontation was now becoming the ultimate game of

146

life and death - be killed or kill. The silence in the room was overpowering as the dark-haired gunmen started his draw.

Chapter 29

After all the outlaws had stood, they slowly fanned out across the saloon. The two in the center were close enough together for both of them to take the double-ought buckshot from this distance in between us so that is where I fired both barrels as soon as the dark-haired gunman on the left went for his weapon. The sound of the Greener 12-gauge was startling and deafening in such closed quarters, but had its desired effect. The Highlander outlaw who was the third man from the left took the brunt of the discharge in his upper chest and throat before he even attempted to pull his Colt. His body was hurled with such force onto the poker table that it collapsed under his weight. He was down, probably dead and for sure out of the fight.

The second outlaw from the left faired a little better as he was only peppered in the chest and throat with double-ought buckshot; he had not been flung like his compadre, but he still dropped to the floor with mortal wounds and withered in pain. He was down and out of the fight. The Greener 12-gauge had taken out two of my assailants.

The outlaw on the far right was no concern of mine since Timber attacked him and had him on the ground going for his throat.

The dark-haired gunman on the far left who fancied himself a gun hand was the fastest by far and he had cleared leather with both of his pistols. I had immediately dropped the Greener after firing both barrels and palmed my Colt, but my draw was not fast enough to not take a bullet from the dark-haired gunman. The 44 slug caught me high up and in the meaty part of the top of my left shoulder, which spun me around just enough that my first shot from the hip missed the outlaw completely and ricocheted off a brass spittoon just to the left of the outlaw. The awkward spin after being shot saved my life as the gunman's second shot missed and imbedded itself into the top of the bar behind me. My wound didn't affect my right arm and shoulder so I was able to fire off a second shot, which found its home in the top of the chest dead centered just below his throat. Not a heart or head shot, but good enough to drop the gunman to his knees. As he tried in vain to raise his pistol again at me, I fired a third time and this time the slug was planted in the dark-haired gunman's face where his nose used to be. He was dead before the back of his head slammed into the floor.

Timber had killed the outlaw on the far right with his powerful jaws, and the blood from that savage and brutal attack was now spreading slowly across the floor. Timber looked fierce and threatening with the blood of one of our adversaries coating his pure white fur.

All four outlaws that had stood up against us were now dead or dying. Timber came out of the ruckus without a scratch. Now that the shootout in the saloon was done, the pain from my shoulder wound was starting to set in. I quickly reloaded my Colt and with some effort because of my left shoulder not working as it should, I reloaded the Greener 12-gauge in case I needed it again - this fight was far from over. I would not know if the next man that walked through the bat-wing doors of the Alma Saloon would be a friend or foe. I needed to be prepared for the later.

Dropping into a chair after reloading, I needed to see how bad my shoulder wound was. I had to stop the bleeding for this fight was not over by a long shot. McPherson and possibly others had to be across the way inside the O'Brien Mining building. It was highly possible my daughter Jessica, her husband Brody, and Finn O'Brien were being held there.

Timber positioned himself between me and the entrance to the saloon. He instinctively knew I was wounded and there was no doubt in my mind he would sacrifice his life to protect me. Unbuttoning my shirt, I stripped it off, and the blood was still flowing freely from the wound in the top of my left shoulder. Gingerly, I poked and prodded the bullet hole and determined it was not that bad and that no major river that flowed the blood to my heart had been damaged. It was a through and through bullet-hole and given time should heal with no lingering damage other than a scar. Standing and walking behind the bar, I grabbed a bottle of whisky - not to drink - but to disinfect the wound. Pouring it generously over the wounds, I winced as I felt the burning sting. It was as if I had woken a hive of pissed off and angry hornets as the alcohol penetrated the wound. Closing my eyes and hoping I would not pass out, I let the initial agony subside into a tolerable throb. Taking my Bowie knife, I cut off several inches of the front tail of the flannel shirt I was wearing. I cut two smaller strips so I could shove them into the wound to help stop the blood flow. Since the bullet that sliced through had not hit any arteries, after several minutes the flow of blood slowed considerably. I was already putting on my shirt when the barkeep and several other men sheepishly entered the saloon.

The thinning grey-haired barkeep after surveying the carnage that was lying on the floor of his saloon slowly made his way until he was standing in front of me. "Marshal Robert, I am astonished that one man could put down four men in such close quarters all by himself."

Looking at the barkeep as I pointed at the yellow-eyed white wolf I replied, "I had help; without Timber it would have been me lying in a puddle of blood. What is your name?"

The barkeep's eyes had landed on Timber after I pointed at him as he answered my question, "Jack Turner."

Jack seemed almost as if he was in a trance. The coppery smell of blood was now saturating the air and overpowering the smell of stale whiskey and the stench from the outhouse just outside the back door of the Alma saloon. I didn't have time to diddle dawdle around and I spoke in a harsher tone, "Jack, look at me. I need you to go fetch the sheriff of Alma."

Jack's eyes blinked several times as his mind was adjusting to the bloodshed of the aftermath of my shootout with the Highlander outlaws. After a couple of nods of his head and several seconds he finally said, "Sheriff King is not in town. He had to take a prisoner to Fairplay for trial. The sheriff does not have a deputy."

That explained why the sheriff and or his deputy had not shown immediately after the shoot-out. That also meant whoever waited for me behind the closed doors of the O'Brien Mining Company was for Timber and I to face alone with no help from the local law. I guess it was fated to be this way; in my mind, I knew it would eventually play out like this. The good news was if Alistair McPherson and others were hiding out in the O'Brien Mining Company, they did not feel confident in their numbers to spare a few men to reinforce those outlaws stationed in the saloon.

Jack was still standing and looking a little bewildered in front of me. I spoke loud and clear so there would be no misunderstanding, "Jack, I need you to clear the streets in between the Alma Saloon and the O'Brien Mining Company. I believe my daughter Jessica, her husband Brody, and Brody's father Finn are being held captive beyond those closed doors. I intend to free them and kill all those that threaten my family. I don't want anyone not involved with this to get shot. Do you understand Jack?"

Jack took several seconds to let my words sink in, but as soon as they did, the barkeep jumped into action and raced out the door and I could hear him as he shouted out to clear the streets. Those townsfolk that had gathered in what they thought was a finished gunfight took flight and found safety behind the walls of the houses and businesses in town. Every one of them was brave until the idea of catching a ricochet or a stray bullet was possible, and then they scattered like chickens from a fox in a hen house.

As the sounds of the fleeing townsfolk faded, silence overcame the night. The blood that drenched Timber's white coat had not been cleaned yet by the white wolf. He looked like a hound from hell and had acted like one - and that is exactly what I needed to finish this fight. He knows that cleaning himself was a waste of time for now since he understood we were not done in our quest for justice and a reckoning.

As I stood, so did Timber. Looking at the yellow-eyed cur, I realized how fortunate that Connor, Veronica, and I had been to have had him on the trail as not only a companion, but that of a furious fighter. When I looked at Timber, he seemed anxious and willing as I spoke to him, "Timber my good fellow, I am not sure of how many there are or of victory against those that stand against us, but one thing I know it is the righteous thing to do. Let's go kill us a Scottish asshole!"

Chapter 30

Pushing through the bat-wing doors, I stepped out onto the boardwalk in front of the Alma Saloon holding the reloaded 12-gauge shotgun. I fully expected to be shot from ambush from the building across the street that housed the O'Brien Mining Company. No shot rang out. As I stood out in the open and in the darkness with Timber the yellow-eyed wolf standing by my side, almost total silence met us. The townsfolk that had come in the aftermath of the shoot-out in the Alma Saloon had vanished from the main street when the barkeep had told them this ordeal and the war being fought in their town was not over. Everyone was curious about hangings and shootouts as long as they were not the one getting hung or shot at.

The wound in my upper left shoulder had stopped bleeding and was forgotten as I had more urgent matters to concern my thoughts.

The almost full moon overhead in the cloudless sky was raining down more than enough light to see the building across the street.

The moon and the night also created more shadows that could hide a man than I would have liked.

The odds were not stacked in Timber's and my favor; I had no illusion that we would survive the night. We had been lucky so far, but now my enemy knew that we were here and exactly where we stood. There would be no parlay and no prisoners. I knew that being righteous was just a notion and would not slay my enemies; that was left up to fate and destiny and how fast and how straight I could shoot.

Feeling a slight colder breeze from the north, I could almost feel the cold and snow of the old man winter that was not far off. As I looked at Timber, he returned my gaze with a look that almost said, "What are we waiting for?"

Never thought I would think of a wolf as almost human, but Timber seemed more human to me at this moment than a lot of folks I had known in my life. Other than Matt Lee, I could not think of anyone I would rather have by my side in such a moment as this. The white wolf was an extraordinary creature in all aspects. He was a loving, loyal, and kind protector of Connor when the situation warranted it. He was also savage, bloody, and a man killer when the need arose. It would seem that Timber and I had more in common than I would care to admit. We were both kin to the wild, dangerous, and adventurous Rocky Mountain Frontier. We were both man killers! We were both predators! Stepping down the three steps from the boardwalk into the dirt street, Timber and I moved as if we were one and the same.

Walking toward the darkened O'Brien Mining Company, I held the Greener shotgun in my right hand just above my Colt riding on my right hip. I felt that I was being watched not only from inside the building owned my Connor's other grandpa, but also by as many of the townsfolk that could see main street from their windows from the safety behind their walls of their businesses and homes. Tonight what was left of the Highlander Gang versus Timber and me was the only show in town.

Halfway across the road, I was starting to feel maybe I had been wrong about McPherson holding my daughter, her husband, and father-in-law hostage in the O'Brien Mining Company. Suddenly a shot rang out and kicked up dirt in front of me followed by a loud voice with a foreign accent, "Hold your ground, Marshal. You and that wolf of yours stop right there."

Both Timber and I came to a halt and stopped as the voice from the shadows wanted. I could not fathom why Alistair McPherson had not just shot me dead where I stood. Obviously he could have, but he had not.

Several seconds went by and nothing more was forthcoming from the darkened building in front of me, and frankly it was starting to piss me off. Speaking loudly and clearly so there was no misunderstanding, "McPherson, we have come to a point that it is now just between you and me! Let my daughter and her family go; they have nothing to do with this. If this was only about the $100,000 you would have gotten it from Finn and left town by now. I am betting that you want some revenge on me for killing that black-hearted bastard who was your brother. If it is a showdown you want, I reckon I am willing and able to give you one. Show yourself and let's end it here and now!"

Another minute passed before the front door opened slowly and a man appeared holding my daughter Jessica in front of him as to shield himself from me. He had his Colt pressed hard into the right side of her head below her ear. Even from this distance in the night, I could see the wetness on her face from the tears she had shed. Whomever this man was, I would kill him for that. The outlaw holding my daughter hostage moved down the boardwalk to the left of me as two more outlaws appeared from the front door with Brody and Finn O'Brien. The O'Brien's, by the looks of them, had been both beaten severely by their captors. They both were being held in front of the outlaws with guns pressed to their heads as well. Then Alistair McPherson stepped through the door, holding a lighted kerosene lamp in his left hand, presumably to keep his right hand, which was his gun hand free. He stood there in all of his arrogance and swagger knowing that he had the upper hand in what was about to happen.

Looking at the man's eyes that held my daughter, I spoke to Jessica, "Jess, It will be okay. Connor is safe and sound just outside of town. This will all be over soon."

My daughter, although distressed with all this ordeal, was still my daughter. She spoke with no quiver in her voice, "Dad, promise me you will kill every one of these sons of bitches even if it means my family's death! Promise me!"

Hearing my daughter's bold statement made me proud as a smile crossed my face. She was tough as nails just like her mother. Her husband and father-in-law obviously had fought their captors for them to take the beating that they had. That made me proud of them. Alistair McPherson thought he had the upper hand, but what he did not know was I was beyond worrying about dying and there was no way in hell that he or his men would walk away tonight! I would kill them all or die trying! I swore that oath to myself as I spoke to my daughter once again in a loud and clear voice, "Jess, you have my word that none of these men walk away from here tonight. They will have to be carried. That is my promise!"

Alistair McPherson laughed out loud once he heard my boast of killing them all. "Seems like bold talk from an over-the-hill and out-gunned old man. I have to admit though you have sand and more pride than most for an old codger. That pride will get you and your whole family dead. After I kill you Marshal, I will kill your daughter, son-in-law, and his daddy. Once that is done, I will capture that pretty young granddaughter of yours again and sell her to the Mexican bandits - a fate worse than death. No one, not even a lawman, gets a free ride for killing any relation of mine. Time to pay the freight for killing my brother!"

As I looked at the three hostages, I knew that no one would live through the night if McPherson had his way. He was set on his revenge for my killing his no account brother. There was no avoiding this showdown and people, maybe my people, would die tonight. Three of the remaining outlaws were using my kin as shields, but McPherson was standing all by his lonesome holding up the kerosene lamp. Those on each side of the Scottish outlaw were far enough away they should not catch any buckshot. No more talk, no more threats, now was the time to start the dance.

Timber must have sensed my thoughts, for he immediately went into a sprint after the outlaw holding Jessica. Knowing the distance was further than I would have liked for a kill shot, I lifted my Greener double-barrel shotgun and pointed in the general direction of McPherson and pulled both triggers. The deafening crack of thunder exploded from the shotgun as I peppered the Scottish renegade with double ought buckshot. Alistair McPherson went down hard onto his back from the force of the shotgun blast dropping the kerosene lamp shattering the glass and spilling the oil. Kerosene oil and fire spread quickly across the boardwalk and the exterior front door and wall of the O'Brien Mining Company.

The outlaw holding Jessica had shoved her in the direction of the blood stained white wolf trying to avert Timber's attack. It cost him his life. Timber easily side stepped Jessica's falling body and sprang with the wolf's glistening white teeth showing themselves in a savage snarl onto the man taking him off his feet. The yellow-eyed wolf had the man's throat within his powerful jaws. With four savage yanks the outlaw's throat separated from his body as he died drowning in his own blood.

The sudden attack by Timber and the thunderous blast of the Greener shotgun had caught the outlaws momentarily off-guard. It helped me that they also saw their boss go down hard giving me the edge I needed to bring the battle to them. With McPherson down for now and Timber engaging the outlaw that had Jessica, I now turned my attention to the remaining two. Dropping the Greener, I palmed my Colt and fired once at the outlaw holding Brody over Brody's shoulder with the bullet penetrating his forehead dropping him like a sack of potatoes. He was stone dead before he fully crumpled onto the burning boardwalk. Thankfully, he had not squeezed the trigger killing my son-in-law.

Brody, now freed from the renegade's grip, moved quickly and ran to and gathered up Jessica into his arms as I turned my full attention to the remaining outlaw holding Jessica's father-in-law at gun point. Finn O'Brien was a tad taller than the Highlander outlaw which gave me no opening in shooting him over Finn's shoulder like I had over Brody's.

Finn, the cagey old man, knew he needed to create an opening, and he did. He simply fell down. The outlaw lost his grip when Finn fell to the ground and I fired three rounds into the outlaw's chest killing him as he was still standing before he flopped over backwards into the now raging fire on the boardwalk.

With only two shells left in my Colt, I turned back toward McPherson. The fire had thirsted on the dry wood, and the front of the building was now fully engulfed in flames. The flickering fire and dancing shadows made it hard to see, but one thing for sure was Alistair McPherson's body was no longer on the boardwalk.

While I searched the street, all I could see through the light of the dancing flames of the burning building was that he was nowhere to be found. Alistair McPherson, the Scottish outlaw, had disappeared.

Looking at Jessica, Brody and Finn, I shouted above the now roaring flames, "Did anyone see where McPherson crawled off to! He was wounded and could not have gotten very far; did anyone see where he went?"

Nobody answered and from the look of confusion, I would say that all three were in a state of shock. A near death experience had a way of doing that to a person. From being held hostage, almost shot, and now their place of business burning out of control, it had left them dumbfounded for now. It would appear nobody saw what happened to the Highlander outlaw. I was almost beside myself.

Searching to no avail and no matter how many times Timber and I paced back and forth in front of the burning O'Brien Mining Company, I could not locate Alistair McPherson alive or dead. It was as if the Scottish outlaw never existed. The heat from the fire caused by the broken kerosene lamp was so intense now that all the townsfolk now gathering on Main Street had to back all the way across the road so their skin would not blister.

After the shootout in front of the O'Brien Mining Company, the townsfolk had started running a bucket brigade to try to quell the fire. The building was totally engulfed and now was threatening the rest of the town. Everyone abandoned their efforts on trying to the save the O'Brien Mining Company building and concentrated on saving the adjacent buildings. It was total chaos in Alma as the fire raged out of control. People were running here and there shouting out orders on how to battle the blaze. Jessica, Brody, and Finn had finally come somewhat to their senses and were now helping the folks of Alma try to save the rest of the town.

Exhaustion of all that had happened tonight finally overcame me and I became dizzy and sat down hard on the boardwalk in front of the Alma saloon. My shoulder wound had started to bleed again, and I felt lightheaded. Timber, knowing I was close to passing out, stood by me as if to guard me in case I did finally succumb to the exhaustion. Knowing I needed to reload, I fumbled with the cartridges and dropped several before finally reloading my Colt. The fire, smoke, and the sound of crackling and the hissing of burning wood filled the night air. Dancing shadows from the thirsty flames played havoc with my night vision.

Having dropped my Greener shotgun after firing at McPherson, I had lost track of it during the ensuing gunfight with the other three outlaws. I had no idea where it was now. All that consumed my mind was, "Where the hell was McPherson? Had he crawled dying into the burning building to escape me? Had I actually shot and wounded him with the shotgun? Was he still alive waiting for the right moment to fulfill his revenge on me and my family?"

My wound, the blood loss, the fatigue of battle, and the over-tiredness of the last couple of weeks had clouded my mind. The people of Alma had all but forgotten about me as they hurried about trying to save the town from the savage fire that had already collapsed the O'Brien Mining Company building. As my mind swirled about trying to put the details of the shootout in the Alma saloon and the battle to save my family in front of the O'Brien building, I did not see Veronica and Connor. They must have made their way into town after the fire started. Connor dismounted her horse and ran into my arms; her tears tried to clean the ash and soot that had settled onto my forearms. Lots of tears, but too much ash. I was rank with the smell of burnt wood and wood ash. My shoulder wound dripped blood. Connor was speaking, for I saw her lips moving as she looked into my eyes. In my confused state I had lost my hearing and could not make out what she was so urgently trying to say.

Veronica sat down next to me and pulled my head onto her shoulder, and I could feel a tear drop silently on my cheek as she tried to comfort me in my obvious distress of the night. Timber stood off a few feet, guarding his family. With Connor on my right side with her head now tucked under my shoulder and Veronica on my left side with my head on her shoulder, I felt that I was home. Still worried about the disappearance of Alistair McPherson, I could no longer think straight and the fatigue and blood loss finally won out, and I slipped slowly into the darkness.

Chapter 31

The "caw, caw" of a Magpie pierced the darkness, and I tried to focus in on the sound of the bird which had to be close. My eyes fluttered and once they opened, I had to shut them again immediately for the light coming in through the window was too intense and it hurt. Actually, everything hurt. All I could feel was pain throughout my whole body. The pain was annoying, but not as much as that damn "caw" bellowing from the Magpie sitting in the aspen tree just outside my window. I hate Magpies.

Slowly opening my eyes once again just to let a pinhole of light filter in, I let them adjust to the daylight. It would seem I had passed out on the boardwalk of the Alma Saloon after my daughter's family business had burnt to the ground. Looking about my room, I was not familiar with my surroundings. Whoever's room this was, they had finished it nicely and seemed to have set me up in a feather bed with fluffy feather pillows. This was more comfort than I was accustomed to and had ever had in my entire life. If not for the agony of my body hurting and that annoying jabber of the Magpie, I could get used to this.

The constant "caw" of the magpie was making my head hurt worse than it already did. Rolling my stiff legs over the side of the bed, I faced the window that was open to a very warm, almost winter day and I could see the black and white of my nemesis, the Magpie. I spied my holster with my Colt hanging on a wooden rocker across the room. If not for the fact that I thought I would probably pass out trying to obtain my weapon to rid myself from the demon bird, I would have shot the annoying Magpie.

There was, however, a small pitcher half-filled with water next to a wash pan sitting on the table next to my bed and within grasp of my hand. Emptying the pitcher into the washbasin, I splashed some cool water on my face and it felt so good. My lips were chapped and cracked, and I wondered how that happened so fast since last night. With the pitcher in my hand, I hefted it to gauge the weight and how much strength it would take to toss it through the window at the black and white devil bird. Now that I was awake, it seemed the Magpie knew I was irritated and was sounding off with its full lung capacity just to exasperate me. It would seem I would have to owe someone a new water pitcher as I brought the porcelain pitcher above my shoulder so I could toss it at my black and white foe. Just as I was about to let loose with the greatest toss in all of history, my bedroom door opened and Veronica, Timber, and Connor walked in. Veronica saw me, the window, and the magpie and quickly put two and two together and said in a quiet, but harsh tone, "Eric Robert, you put that pitcher down!"

Having been caught in the act of trying to murder the bird, I quickly set the water pitcher down and raised my eyebrows and gave Veronica, Timber, and Connor my best "ah shucks" shrug, which in doing so caused a shooting pain in my wounded shoulder. I guess I sort of deserved it.

Veronica stood with her hands on her hips giving me the stink eye for even thinking about throwing the pitcher at the Magpie. I could not help but notice that Veronica was looking even more beautiful than the last time I saw her.

Timber the yellow-eyed wolf had cleaned himself up since the night of our confrontation with the Highlander gang. His almost white of snow fur was no longer matted with blood of our enemies.

He seemed happy to see me and wagged his tail back and forth like a normal dog would.

Connor's eyes got big and her face lit up with a huge smile as she looked back and forth from Veronica to me in our silent stare down and started to laugh. Not just a giggle, but a wholehearted laugh that showed the happiness of my one and only granddaughter. Hearing her enjoyment made me laugh, and that made Veronica laugh.

Veronica went to the window as Connor moved toward me. Veronica waved her arms several times shooing the Magpie away, which was almost as satisfying as if I had been able to bing it on the noggin with a water pitcher. Almost...

Connor and Timber both jumped into bed with me and snuggled up close, and Connor said with glee in her voice, "It is about time you woke up, Grandpa!"

Holding my granddaughter as tight as my sore arms could hold, I looked out the window and gauged the time of day and decided by the shadows on the ground of the building across the way it had to be close to noon. Smiling at Connor, I said, "I don't believe in my whole life I have ever slept a night away until noon the next day."

Connor looked baffled, and I wondered whether maybe it was even later in the day. I looked to Veronica as she pulled up the wooden rocker and sat down just in front of Connor and myself. Veronica reached out and gently touched me and said in that quiet voice of hers, "Not just a night until noon, Marshal. You have been out for six nights and a half of a day. We were starting to worry that you may have sustained some sort of injury to your brain and would never wake up." Six nights and a half a day! No wonder my body was so stiff and sore and my lips were dry and chapped. Looking at Connor who now had a worried look on her face, I said with a half chuckle, "Guessing I was a tad tired from all that running around."

That seemed to please Connor, and she smiled back and said, "Mom said you were just playing possum and was getting lazy on us."

That brought another round of laughter from Veronica, Connor, and myself. Looking out the window, I tried to recall what happened that night almost a week ago. Running it through my thinker, I remembered the most important aspect of what had transpired. Looking to Veronica I asked, "Did anyone find the body of Alistair McPherson?"

Veronica's eyes kind of clouded over and she shook her head "no" before she started to speak, "No, his body and his horse have seemed to have disappeared. Finn thinks after you hit him with the shotgun, he crawled back into the building and succumbed to his wounds. Finn also reasoned that the fire was so hot and intense that his body was all consumed by the inferno and cremated him completely to ash. Several of the outlaw horses plus some town horses panicked in the fire's melee and ran off. Some including Alistair's horse are still missing. Everyone is in an agreement that is what happened to McPherson and his horse. Everyone thinks that each and every one of the Highlander gang is dead and got what they richly deserved. Believe me Eric, you could run for Mayor and everyone in town would vote for you. The whole town has been worried about you and have had nightly prayer meetings at the church in your honor."

Thinking about it for a spell, I know that McPherson had taken most if not all the buckshot from the Greener shotgun. If he had lived through the initial blast and was wounded, it made sense he would have crawled into the building to get out of shooting range. The fire would have just been started and the building would have been his only safe haven at that moment in his wounded condition. I had seen cremated remains of men before, and there have been always bone fragments left behind but if you did not know what you were looking for, you might not recognize them for what they were. Once I was able, I would visit the burnt out building myself and have a look see. As for the horses running off scared, that even made more sense to me. Since it had almost been a week since the fire and shootout, it would seem plausible that is exactly what happened. It was more than likely that I had mortally wounded Alistair McPherson, and his body was destroyed by the fire. It still bothered me that no one was a hundred percent sure though.

Veronica spoke as I was thinking, "You need to rest Eric and put all of this behind you for now. I am sure you are hungry and I got some venison stew ready with some Dutch oven biscuits. I will go fetch a bowl for both of you seeing how Connor seems to be settled in all nice and comfortable in that feather bed."

Connor looked up at me and still with that face splitting grin said, "This is a pretty comfortable bed isn't it, Grandpa? This is mom and dad's bed, and I enjoy sleeping in here when they will let me."

Bringing my granddaughter in close, I realized how lucky I was to have her grace my life. Everything that Matt Lee and I went through to bring her home to give her a chance at a decent life was worth it. Matt Lee knew in his heart it was his last good offering in this world, and it saddened me to think of my friend who gave his life so Connor could live hers. Releasing Connor I said, "It is that and much more. Hope I don't get spoiled sleeping in such a fine feather bed. Sweetheart, I need you to do me a favor and search my pocket of my vest that is over there on top of the dresser. Look to see if there is a folded letter in the pocket."

Connor did as I asked and within minutes she was back with the letter. Matt Lee's letter that contained his last words to Walk With Ghost now smelled of wood smoke. It was amazing with all that had happened, I still had it and it was still in one piece. Without opening it or reading it, I brought the letter up to my lips and speaking almost in a whisper to no one in particular I said, "Ghost, I will do as I promised and as soon as I am able, I will take this letter of love to be buried with your wife. It is the least I can do for all that you did for me and mine!"

Chapter 32

The next three days slowly passed as I healed up from my shoulder wound. It was a wonderful time and finally I felt at home with my daughter Jessica, Brody, Finn, and granddaughter Connor. Finn and Brody O'Brien took up the task of clearing the burnt-out shell of their business so they could rebuild their offices again. It would seem that money was no object as they purchased enough wood and materials that would be delivered by wagons so their team of fourteen carpenters could begin building a replacement office bigger and better than the one that had been destroyed in the fire.

Before the O'Brien's team of laborers began clearing the rubble, Finn gave Timber and me the chance to walk the wreckage looking for any telltale evidence that the raging inferno had consumed Alistair McPherson's body. I spent almost a full day sifting through the ruins looking for bone fragments and such. The fire had been intense and left mostly ash and soot. Nothing I could find seemed to me like bone fragments or anything resembling a skeleton or the body of a man. I was thinking it was destiny for me to never know exactly what happened to McPherson that night. Although I had no evidence that said he was dead, I knew I had shot him with a 12 gauge double-ought buckshot. If he did in fact survive the initial blast and was able to get away, he was more than likely mortally wounded and had succumbed to his wounds somewhere else. Just like Veronica told me the night before, it was time I quit worrying about Alistair McPherson. He had to be dead.

Once I was fully healed, the weather took a turn for the worse and it snowed for two days. It was a wonderful time spent with my O'Brien family and Veronica. Timber lay by the fire for several days as the snow continued as I had seen him do at Ghost's cabin in Redemption Valley. It would seem that the white haired wolf had found a forever home. We ate and told stories around the fireplace as Jessica, Connor, and Veronica made the most delicious meals and baked goods such as my favorite apple pie.

My love that had been established on the trail from Phantom Canyon to Alma for Veronica flourished. Of course, falling in love takes two people; if it is one-sided then it is most often a very sad affair. It would seem Veronica felt the same for me, and I can't remember anything this special ever happening to me. At my age, I had given up any hope or even any thought of having a woman that I loved with all my heart by my side. Of course the lady of my desire was a tad younger than I was, and her dark brown hair was almost always tied into one pigtail that fell about a foot below her shoulders. Although Veronica Flores was slender and small in stature, she was not frail. As I watched Veronica walk or move, she had the determination and the grace of one of those fancy ballerina dancers. Veronica was always catching me looking at her, because I was always looking at her. Her deep dark brown eyes had a way of catching the flicker of the fireplace light and it never failed to stir my blood. There was no doubt that Veronica Flores was a strong, independent and fine-looking woman. I was so in love with this woman; now I knew how Ghost felt toward his wife Walk With Ghost.

I was almost scared of asking Veronica to share my life and marry me. In reality, I had nothing to offer her. I was an aging Federal Marshal with no place I could really call home. If I retired today, I would receive a small retirement pension. Very small. I had no home, land, cattle, gold or money to speak of. All I had to offer was all of my love that I could muster; I wondered if it was enough. I was not sure I was worthy of someone such as Veronica Flores. I believed she deserved more in life than some aging lawman. I would have to ponder on it more before I actually asked her.

Being isolated in Jessica and Brody's house during the snowstorm had made me antsy and had given me cabin fever. Not that I didn't love Jessica, Brody, and Connor, but I was a man for the wild trail of the Rocky Mountain frontier anytime of the year. I needed the fresh air that was beneath the sun and the moon. I needed to be out in the wilderness, and I felt the urge to fulfill my promise to Matt Lee to deliver his letter to his wife. I was afraid if I waited much longer that the winter and any more accumulation of snow would make the trek into Redemption Valley impossible. Hell, it might already be impossible.

Having decided to move on to finish my quest and promise to Matt Lee, I now would have to face the quandary of asking Veronica to marry me. I could not leave knowing that she might not be here when I got back. My plan was to ask her outright after supper tonight when she joined me on the outside deck as I smoked my evening pipe of tobacco.

Supper went by painfully slow and the antsier I got. Jessica, Connor, and Veronica were enjoying each other's company and were talking up a storm like no other. Brody had retired for the night and headed for bed. I tried to wait out the girls as they talked about their lives with each other, but I started to sweat and started to lose my nerve in asking the woman I dreamed of to be my wife. Actually, I was getting sore at myself because none of this was going like I had planned. I thought that maybe in just a couple of more minutes that they possibly could not find another subject to converse about, but their conversation rolled into another hour. Finally, I could not stand the pressure anymore and I stood up and mumbled, "Excuse me."

My words had no effect, and the girls kept it up with the mouths flapping as if I was not even in the room. Taking my fist, I pounded on the table hard enough to knock over the salt shaker when I said more forcibly, "Excuse me, I got something I need to say!"

That got their attention, and they all stopped talking and looked at me with wide eyes wondering what the heck had gotten into me. Quickly I righted the salt shaker and pointed at the table where I had pounded my fist. "I…hmmmmm, sorry about all that. It is just that I got something eating at my craw, and I need to get it out or I will never say it. Getting antsy holding it in."

Definitely had their attention now. I was looking at the three women who meant the most to me in life. Jessica had the look as if I had stepped on her toes with my boot. Connor and Veronica had looks of amusement on their faces as I cleared the lump out of my throat and in a quavering voice, "I guess I would rather face a whole gang of outlaws again than face the three of you this way. Sometimes life puts you in a position that you just have to go for it even if it makes you look like a fool. This would be one of them times, so here it is."

Walking on unsteady legs around the table, I stood above Veronica as I looked into her dark eyes and took a moment before speaking to bask in the warmth and the love I felt for this woman. Finally, clearing my voice once again, I finally got the courage to speak. "Veronica, I have to finish my promise to Matt Lee, and I will be leaving tomorrow to do so. I can't ride away from here, even for a few days, without knowing that you will be here waiting for me to return. I am not much to look at, nor do I have anything of real value to offer. I have no home I can call my own, I have no gold, cattle, property, and very little cash. Most times I speak before I think which more often than not is not good. That being said, I am sure of what I am about to say. Once we were on the trail after leaving Phantom Canyon, I dreamed of you. Since we have been here safe in Alma these past days, I no longer dream of you because getting to know you better in life is way better than those dreams I had in the beginning. Being in love with you makes my sunsets and sunrises brighter and more meaningful. I guess Veronica, what I am stumbling around to here is that I want you to be my wife. Will you marry me?"

Jessica and Connor teared up with the emotion of the moment, but not Veronica. Veronica's smile never left her face as she sat for a moment or two and studied my face before she spoke. "I was wondering if or when you would ask Eric. You are all the man that any woman would want and just the one man that makes me take a deep breath each and every time I see you. Of course Eric Robert, I will marry you."

Chapter 33

After only a few hours of sleep, I woke up an hour before dawn, and everyone in the household was still sleeping. Jessica, Connor, Finn, and Veronica stayed up most of the night planning a wedding. Jessica woke up and told Brody, and he went and fetched his dad Finn. Jessica and her father-in-law had taken the reins in the affair and were planning a larger wedding than I cared for in the Alma church. Finn O'Brien insisted he was going to pay for the whole shindig as a wedding gift for Veronica and me. After seeing the happiness in the O'Brien household, I reluctantly agreed since Finn kept repeating how I had saved him $100,000. I thought it best to not bring up the fact if not for me his place of business would not have burnt down to the ground.

It would seem everyone, especially Connor, was in agreement that Veronica and I getting hitched was a wondrous affair. After seeing everyone's smiling faces, there was no way I could ever back out now. Not that I wanted to, for just watching Veronica at the supper table last night as the fireplace's dancing shadows lit her face and strengthened my resolve that I knew it was the right decision. She was beyond beautiful and I loved her more than life itself.

The house had already had cooled some since everyone went to bed. One of the gals had packed five pounds of venison jerky, twelve Dutch oven biscuits, four cans of peaches, and leftover fried turkey from last night's supper. In my new grub sack, there also was the leftover apple pie, which I was thankful for. I even located twelve pieces of fudge in the bag. It would seem that I would eat well on the trail to Boreas Pass and Redemption Valley.

I wanted to leave before awakening anyone because I was no good at saying goodbyes. After belting on my holster and checking the loads in my Colt, I reached for my Winchester and hat. I made sure that Matt Lee's letter to his wife was in my vest pocket as I headed to the door.

Walking from the kitchen to the main room of the house, I stopped and before me Connor and Timber were standing waiting on me at the front door on this frosty morning. Connor was still in her flannel nightshirt and her eyes were barely open, and she looked sleepy and sad that I was leaving. My granddaughter, whom I had not met until this whole ordeal with the kidnapping and the Highlander gang, had stolen my heart in less than a month. She was my angel and a drowsy one at that. Looking at her I knew that Matt Lee would have been more than proud of being the reason she was here safe at home. Connor spoke first, "Timber woke up when he heard you shuffling around the house, Grandpa. He wants to go with you. I want him to go with you."

Crouching down so I was eye level to my granddaughter, I reached out and pulled her in for a hug and she lay her head on my shoulder when I said in a quiet voice, "I most appreciate you wanting to send Timber with me Connor, but his place is here with you now. This is his home now, and he cherishes you. I think he probably wants to stay."

Connor pushed out with her arms so she could look me in the eyes, and I saw her deep concern. She spoke in a voice just barely above a whisper, "This is Timber's home and I know he is my wolf, but he loves the wild and you, Grandpa. You and Timber are one and the same. He needs to go on this trip with you to Redemption Valley; just like you he needs to say his goodbyes to

Ghost and Walk With Ghost. I had a dream last night and something bad will happen if Timber does not go."

Connor, in all of her innocence of childhood, had worried about Timber's feelings in losing his friendship with Ghost. It touched my heart that she saw what no one else could see. She was right; Timber had to make the trip. It would be good for both of us, and I would enjoy his company. Wiping the sole tear that had formed in my eye, I brought Connor back in close and spoke to her, "Nothing bad will happen to me my little one. You saw that Timber needed to ease his grief as I do in losing Matt Lee. He can go, knowing full well that - if he had a mind to - we couldn't have stopped him anyway. We will be back in a week and you can then update me on the wedding plans. I love you, Connor."

Connor pushed back again and looked me in the eyes and I saw no relief in her face. Something was still bothering her. After what had happened to her, I was guessing the thought of the two that protected her leaving for now was worrisome. She looked at me for a long spell with her eyes searching mine before she spoke, "I love you, Grandpa! Just keep Timber close and don't lose sight of him."

Kissing Connor on the forehead, I stood and tried to make light of the matter, and I said with a half-chuckle, "Will do Connor, he can even share my blanket with me just so long as he is not stinking too much from the trail."

Connor slowly backed away and gave Timber a huge hug around his neck, and then she spoke to him in a caring and loving voice, "You go now with grandpa to say goodbye to Ghost. Remember what we talked about, Timber; you need to stay close to Grandpa Eric."

Timber stood as soon as Connor let go of his neck, and he looked her dead in the eye as if he was communicating with Connor in a way that no one else could understand. He stood silently for a few moments before he licked her face and walked over and then sat down at my feet looking up at me with a "let's get on the trail - daylight is burning" look.

After I slipped on my winter coat and then grabbed the grub sack, Timber and I with one last look at Connor stepped out into the cold of the morning. The early air was cold and it bit into my lungs. Turning up the collar of my coat to help keep my neck warm, I thought to myself, "Eric Robert, you are getting old." I reckon since I had been indoors most of the time healing up that I had lost some of my wilderness toughness being in a warm house. It would take me a day or so to get used to the outdoors again. Timber seemed not to be affected by the cold at all and moved quickly to the barn where the horses were.

Deciding of course to ride Gypsy, I chose Spirit to be the pack horse. Seeing how Connor saw that Timber needed to have his last goodbyes, I thought it was only fitting that Ghost's horse Spirit had the same opportunity to ease her grief.

Both Gypsy and Spirit were busy prancing and pawing the ground with their hooves in anticipation of going back on the trail almost to the point it became difficult to saddle them both. Once Gypsy was saddled and I packed away my gear on Spirit, I stepped into the stirrup and planted my behind in the saddle and led both of the horses out of the barn. Timber the yellow-eyed wolf took the lead as if he knew exactly where we were headed. Timber never ceased to amaze me; it would not surprise me if the white-furred wolf knew exactly what trail to take. He would be a pleasure to have on the trail, for both of us now had to complete my promise and our solemn duty to a good man.

The weather seemed as if it would cooperate in this mission to fulfill Ghost's last request. Although cold this morning with about a foot of snow on the ground, the sky was cloudless, and the sun was just now making its appearance over the eastern horizon. It would be a glorious blue and orange sunrise that one never quite got used to here along the Rocky Mountain frontier at this altitude.

As a crow flies it was probably only nine or ten miles northwest to Redemption Valley, but since I was no crow, I would have to skirt the high mountains and take the low road southeast six miles to Southpark into the town of Fairplay. Once there, I would continue on a northwest course for ten miles on the flat plateau of Southpark until I got to Como. Once in Como it was roughly another four miles up the Boreas Pass Trail to Redemption Valley. The snow was going to slow us down, but hopefully I would be able to find the hidden entrance to Redemption Valley by midday tomorrow.

With Timber taking point, I gave Gypsy her head and the reins and we moved out briskly.

Chapter 34

To skirt the high mountains and follow the easy trail, I had to head southeast toward the town of Fairplay. That would put me on the western edge of the South Park high mountain plateau. In South Park the land leveled out fairly nice which on a sunny summer day made traveling easier. The problem, it was not summer. It was now the beginning of winter and if the wind kicked up from the north, then all hell could break loose.

Whiteouts were as common in South Park at 9,000 feet as they were on the eastern plains of Colorado. White normally meant purity as in a new start or new beginnings. White wedding dresses and white picket fences were well meaning, but a whiteout blizzard could have you straddling the fence between life and death. Many a tough man in the mountains had succumbed to the specter of death riding the coattails of a northern blow in South Park. Looking heavenward, I saw the sky above was cloudless and the evergreens that lined the trail stood silently with their branches weighted down from the last snow, but unmoving. For now the wind was staying in the North. After living here my entire life, I knew that could change rapidly at this altitude. Living life along the Rocky Mountain frontier was not for those with a faint heart.

The six mile trail in between Alma and Fairplay was a much-traveled route and the snow that had recently fallen had already been broken by others before me. Timber took the lead, and it was hard to see him as his white full winter coat blended in so well with the snow as nature intended it to be. Timber would race ahead for about 100 feet or so and then turn around and watch and wait for Gypsy, Spirit, and me to catch up. Once we got caught up, he would race ahead again. Watching the yellow-eyed wolf in his natural environment once again reminded me of what a magnificent creature Timber was. Here in the wilderness, he was savagely beautiful.

Gypsy and Spirit were also enjoying the trail and the wilds that surrounded us. It was days like this that made me feel so alive. Good horses and the coldness that stung my face told me I was the envy of all those that lived in those dark and dirty cities back in the eastern states.

As I rode in the silence of the snow, I thought of all that had happened since the Highlander gang had kidnapped Connor. It had been a high adventure that included blood, killing, and death. The cost had been high; my daughter's family business had been burnt to the ground, and the death of Matt Lee weighed heavily on my mind and heart. There had been some good that had come out of it as well. Connor would get a chance to live her life. Then an asset I had never dreamed about had come in the very shapely form of Veronica Flores. Veronica would soon be my wife. Who would have ever thought it?

As I pondered on all the recent memories be them good or bad, I felt that the whole kidnapping and Highlander gang ordeal was undone. It was worrisome to me that the body of Alistair McPherson had never been found. I knew probably the outlaw had died from his wounds after I had shot him with my 12-gauge shotgun, but it still nagged at me that there was still a possibility he was alive. That last thought sent a cold chill spinning out of control through my body as if a ghost had passed on through. Pulling gently back on Gypsy's reins, I brought her to a halt and turned in my saddle and looked at my back trail and saw nothing but snow and evergreens. My gut feeling was someone was following me. Shaking my head to clear it, I pondered for a spell and then whispered to myself, "You are getting old, senile, and scary Eric Robert!" Touching the letter from my friend to his wife in my vest pocket as if to remind me of the task at hand, I gave Gypsy her head and the reins and moved on toward Fairplay.

There was no reason for me to stop in Fairplay, so I just rode past it on the trail that headed northeast toward Como. The flat and unbroken snow before me on the high plateau of South Park caught the morning sun and twinkled like the stars in the night sky. It was a sight to behold that was for sure. The snow here was only four inches deep and had yet to be drifted by the northern winds which made our trek across this winter landscape almost enjoyable. Timber was still taking the lead and running ahead, enjoying this outing as if he knew what awaited at the end of the trail for us.

At midday we stopped at Trout Creek that was still running clear so we didn't have to break any ice to get our fill of some fresh water. My stomach was doing some grumbling since I had not thought to eat breakfast before leaving Alma. While watching my back trail as the horses and Timber got a drink, I devoured three Dutch oven biscuits and a half of a pound of the turkey that was in my grub sack. Timber watched me and I tossed him some turkey and a couple of biscuits, and he wolfed them on down. Laughing, I said to my yellow-eyed companion, "You are getting soft, Timber. It would seem being around people has domesticated you some. Before when I first saw you, you were the king of the mountain. Hell, now son you are nothing more than a big lap dog."

Timber moved in closer as he helped me study our back trail. Silently I ate two pieces of fudge and gave Timber a couple of pieces as well. We watched behind us for another quarter click of an hour and I wondered if Timber had the same gut feeling that I had that something or someone was behind us?

Seeing nobody behind us and nobody on the trail in front of us, we pushed on to Como. Looking northwest, I could see a snowstorm raging on top of Mount Silverheels and a tad further east on Little Baldy Mountain; both mountains topped out above timberline and ole' man winter savagely pushed his dominance on top of those mountains. Here at 9000 feet on the floor of South Park, the wind was still not present and the temperature had risen enough to make it comfortable enough that I had taken off my winter coat and was down to a flannel shirt over my long johns.

The warmth of the sun during the day was now slowly waning as the sun started its arc below the western horizon. By my reckoning the town of Como was just a little over a mile to the north. Once again, there was no reason to stop. I had plenty of grub and the weather was as good as it gets this time of the year, so I located a suitable place to make a camp.

After building a comfortable fire, I saw to the horses and their needs. After unpacking and unsaddling them, I gave Gypsy and Spirit both a good going over with my wooden curry comb. Once that was done, I gave them both a generous helping of grain from my supplies and both got a treat of sugar. The whole time I was grooming and feeding the horses, Timber stood by my side and watched our back trail. Crouching down so I was at Timber's height, I reached out and lay my hand on his muscular back and gave him some loving caresses as we both now studied the trail behind us. It was now clear to me that the white wolf felt uneasy. "Well, Timber my friend, I guess you feel it. Things are not like what they seem to be. I am thinking you have that gut feeling as I do that something or someone is behind us. It could be as simple as someone traveling the same trail as we are or a mountain lion hunting supper, but my instinct is telling me differently. I feel we are being followed and hunted, and not by a critter."

After moving the horses closer to the fire, I palmed my Colt and loaded a round in the empty chamber that usually I kept empty for safety. You never know what might come out of the dark tonight. Holstering the Colt, I grabbed my Winchester and the grub sack and headed for the warmth of the fire and Timber followed me.

After setting up my bedroll for the night, Timber and I finished up the rest of the turkey and Dutch oven biscuits. For dessert I ate a can of peaches and to my surprise so did my wolf companion. Timber made me laugh out loud several times as he tried to lick the sweet juice out of the can. His snout was larger than the can itself and made for a comical effort on Timber's part as he finally got it done and licked the inside of the can dry.

After I dropped a few more logs on the fire to keep it going long enough to have some good coals in the morning, Timber and I shared my bedroll for each other's body heat. My Winchester was under the flannel blankets as well and the Colt was within an easy grasp under my saddle which I was using to rest my head on. Knowing Timber's eyes, ears, and sense of smell were way better than mine, I fell asleep quickly.

Chapter 35

My eyes snapped open. It was still dark, but something had awakened me. Lying still for several seconds, I tried to gather my senses of all that surrounded me. Timber was no longer sleeping next to me and sitting up slowly, I let my eyes adjust to the darkness and the very faint orange and red shimmering light from the still hot embers of the fire. Timber was sitting up and staring into the darkness in the direction that we had traveled. His hackles were not up and he was just sitting there watching our back trail as if he was waiting patiently. Gypsy and Spirit were close enough I could see both of them in the low light of the remaining campfire and the half-moon above. Neither horse seemed alarmed. Whatever was out in the dark was far enough away still that it had only sparked Timber's curiosity and nothing more. Knowing Timber was watching the camp, I rolled back on my side after pulling up the blankets tighter to my chin for warmth and fell back asleep.

The next time I woke up, it was the sounds of horses neighing riding the mountain breeze from Como just about a mile away. The sky to the east had lightened some as the day was in its infancy. What had kept Timber interested during the night must have moved on since he was now sleeping soundly next to me, but on top of my bedroll. Moving slowly as not to disturb Timber's slumber, I stood and tried to ease my muscles back into life. I had gotten used to sleeping in a goose feather bed back in Alma and it had softened me up some. Or maybe it was I was just getting old, and the hard ground and the cold were tougher on my old bones. Whatever the issue was, I was stiff and sore this morning as I started stirring the leftover embers from last night to coax them into a fire large enough to add more kindling. Once the kindling caught hold, I added more wood for a fire big enough to warm my hands over.

After I warmed up and got my blood flowing to all my parts, the ache of the cold hard ground was starting to disappear. Timber and I had a cold breakfast of two pounds of venison jerky brought from Alma and a canteen of cold creek water. The sun was now peeking above the mountains in the east, but the warmth had yet to reach us. After dousing the fire, I made Gypsy and Spirit ready for the trail, and Timber once again took to watching our back trail. It would seem that both of us still felt whatever or whoever was back behind there still. It could be they or it were traveling at the same speed and we were staying just far enough back as not to alarm Timber and the horses. I was getting irritated.

Once planted in the saddle on Gypsy, I touched Ghost's letter to his wife in my vest pocket to make sure I still had it and then I pointed my mare toward the town of Como and gave her a slight jab of my right spur as we moved out. With no need to stop at Como once again, I skirted the edge of the mining settlement, which left a half day's ride to Redemption Valley.

It was not long after passing Como before we were riding past the Como cemetery at the base of Boreas Pass. I stopped about 100 feet back for a few minutes and watched about ten people attending a funeral, and I could not help but wonder how deep the frost had been driven into the ground. The dirt piled up seemed dry and unfrozen yet. Out of respect for the departed, I took my hat off as the mourners said their piece about the virtues of the deceased and sang a few church hymns. When they started in with the song Amazing Grace, I sang it as well; it never failed to bring a tear or two and a flood of memories of all those that I cared for and loved who had passed on. Watching the funeral flooded me with guilt for having to leave the body of Matt Lee there at the mouth of Phantom Canyon during the rescue of Connor and Veronica and the escape from the Highlander Gang. Touching Ghost's letter to Walk With Ghost, I thought it would be fitting for me to sing Amazing Grace once I buried the letter. Knowing my version would be short on melody and strong on noise made me smile knowing if Matt Lee could hear it, he would have as much fun as a baby with a belly ache. That thought made me laugh out loud and Timber gave me the ole' stink eye for laughing at a funeral. I was far enough away it didn't seem to bother the folks all dressed in black though. Once a couple of men started to shovel dirt back into the hole, I gave Gypsy her reins and we moved out and started up the incline of Boreas Pass.

At mid-morning the sun was up high enough that the warmth reached over the evergreens and it felt pleasing on my face. All the clouds above had disappeared, and the breeze was a gentle one as we continued up the pass. Up ahead as I remembered was a very thick stand of aspen and evergreen trees. The snow depth during the first mile was almost nonexistent as if the wind and the snow never reached the ground on this side of the mountain since the evergreens were so thick, heck the sun was having a difficult time finding its way through the thick evergreen needles.

The trail up the pass had not been traveled since the last snow, for the only tracks that could be seen were that of the critters that lived upon the mountain - elk, deer, wolves, rabbits, squirrels and such. No tracks of man or horses and it would seem that on this side of Boreas Pass, we were the only ones foolish enough to try to travel it this far into winter. The good news was I was traveling only another mile or so to the entrance of Redemption Valley. Last time I was here when I asked for Matt Lee's help, it was in the autumn and now with winter here it all looked so different. The first time I was here, the location of the hidden valley was only revealed when I saw a bull elk seemingly disappear into the side of the mountain. There might be a possibility that I might not be able to find it this time.

At midday my gut instinct was telling me I was close. Pulling back on Gypsy's reins, I brought her and Spirit to a halt as I studied the south side of the mountain. I stopped. But Timber moved forward and headed toward the mountain as if he had a purpose. I was smiling now, for it would seem the yellow-eyed wolf knew exactly where we were going and headed for the hidden entrance. Seeing how the white wolf had taken charge, I spurred Gypsy into following him.

Timber waited for Gypsy, Spirit and me to catch up as we started through the veiled entrance of Redemption Valley. Stopping for a minute, I looked at our back trail and saw our tracks; if anyone was tracking us, we just left a nice trail for them to follow. There was not a lot I could do about it, so I pushed that thought off to the side of my mind and followed Timber into the valley that used to be his home. Just as I recalled, the first quarter of a mile was a natural sluice in the shape of "V." Exiting the narrow sluice once again brought us into a wider valley surrounded by mountains in a bowl shape. The grandeur of all before took my breath away, for the valley seemed to be untouched by man, and I could only imagine that it looked like this the day the Lord created the earth. Every mountain that surrounded this valley was well above timberline, and it was my thought the only entrance that could possibly exist was the one I just rode through.

I was close to the end of my quest as we moved into the center of Redemption Valley and found the small stream that flowed west to east as it meandered lazily across the valley floor supplying fresh water to all that lived here within these walls. Here and along the stream, as one would expect, were tracks of all the living creatures that got their water from this creek. Still, there were no tracks of man or any horses.

After another quarter of a mile next to the stream, I found what I was looking for - a simple wooden cross marking the grave of Walk With Ghost, the wife of the legend himself. Bringing Gypsy to a halt, I dismounted to get closer to read the inscription on the marker. The words that had been carved by Matt Lee could still be read, "Walk With Ghost - Ute Indian princess and my wife. Not a day went by that I didn't love her."

Chapter 36

Standing up and still looking at Walk With Ghost's grave marker, I could almost feel the love that Matt must have felt as he carved the epitaph on the wooden cross for his wife. After retrieving a gold miner's pick and shovel that I had packed away for this occasion on Spirit, I went to work as Timber stood by watching me pick and shovel out a hole about two feet deep and a foot wide on top of Walk With Ghost's grave. Feeling I had a deep enough hole to do what needed to be done, I then retrieved a round tin can that used to house cigars that had been given to me by Finn O'Brien back in Alma. My intention when done was to place Matt Lee's final letter in the can and then bury it as he had asked me to do.

Before reading Matt's letter to his wife, I felt the need to speak some of my own words. Clearing my voice and speaking to no one in particular, but the trees and the mountains, "As promised my friend, I have brought your final letter here to be buried with Walk With Ghost. It has humbled me. You trusted in me to do this little thing after all that you did for my granddaughter Connor. I know you never got to meet her, but I assure you Matt, that as long as I live, she will never forget the ultimate sacrifice that you gave so she could live a full life. There is nothing I can say or do that can express my gratitude, but also my sadness. You were a man that lived his life to the fullest, and you bowed to no one. I respected you for that. The warrior in you was the bravest and toughest I had ever seen. The heart that beat within your chest was full of love for these mountains that surround us and for the woman that took you to be her husband. I have met no one that can hold a candle to both of you. It honors me to call you both my friends."

My heart was heavy, and I shed a few tears as I remembered my friends for who they were and what they stood for. Timber felt my grief as he moved in so he was standing close enough to touch my leg to comfort me as I reached into my vest pocket and produced Matt Lee's letter.

I unfolded the letter gently because over the time since Matt Lee had written the letter, it had taken a severe beating. Actually, it amazed me it was still all in one piece. The ink had faded some and the tears that blurred my eyes made it a little challenging to read. Not wanting to stumble over Matt's words when I spoke, I read the letter through all the way twice before feeling confident to read it out loud hoping not to miss a beat. Several of my tears had fallen onto the page, and I worried it might smudge it some. Clearing my throat and the grief that clouded my mind, I began to speak the Ghost's thoughts. "Walk With Ghost, I have been dealing with the grief of your death. I always thought it would be me that would pass on first. I am not prepared to live life without you, and you invade my dreams at night. The love I had for you and no one else still beats within my chest. You were my everything, and you will always be.

It was you that saved me from my own demons and made me into the man I am. I had always been capable of taking care of you and defending you against all the Rocky Mountains had to throw at us - mountain lions, the death of our two boys, cold and snow, outlaws, bounty hunters, renegades, and Indian hatred. I comforted you when our son - your son by blood, mine by love - followed the mountain man trail and headed west. I did my best with all I know to honor, cherish and love you, yet I was not capable enough to stop the sickness that took your life always praying for death to take me instead of you. Our valley, our home is not the same anymore without your grace and laughter. Timber misses you and sleeps most nights at your grave as if he is still protecting you.

You taught me years ago that death cannot take who we love away from us. They are always there in the heart and mind. In your passing I have found this to be true for every day since you died, you have walked beside me unseen and unheard, but I have felt your presence in the trees and the wind. Your spirit and the essence of what you were now lives in the aspens and evergreens and the cool mountain breeze. I can feel your warmth at night within our cabin. You are with me in death - this I know. Won't be long my love, and I will join you. I have one good task and a debt that I need to pay and complete and then I will come home to you.

Oh my love, I have had a vision and it won't be long until I will be by your side for eternity. Our friend Eric Robert has asked the impossible of me. His granddaughter Connor has been kidnapped, and he has asked me to join him to rescue her from the outlaws that have taken her. I cannot refuse since he is the one that gave us the last year of your life to live in peace and harmony. I owe him for that. We are outmanned and outgunned. In the vision I saw the young girl will live. My vision also told me I will not. I am okay with that. For what is my life without you? Without you I am lost and heartbroken. The Marshal has promised to return this letter to Redemption Valley to be buried with you. My body will feed the wolves and the magpies, but my soul is here within these words to be with you."

Your loving husband, Matt.

Looking at the letter for another full minute after reading it, I realized my promise to Matt Lee was now at the end. I felt happiness and sadness at the same time, and both of the emotions were almost overwhelming. Putting Ghost's love letter to his wife into the cigar tin, I quickly buried it. I then made a promise to myself to bring Connor and Veronica next spring to this final resting place of the man that without his help there would have been an unpleasant future for all of us. It was also my thought to bring a better headstone that could withstand the savage winters in this hidden valley.

Standing with Timber by my side, I could feel the wind at our backs as if I was in a funnel as the chilled winter wind rushed northward to the one and only exit - this hidden valley sluice like entrance.

One never knows what the little thing that the Rocky Mountains would create that will be their eventual downfall. On this day it was the strong wind at our back carrying away any scent of danger that may be close and downwind from us. None of us - Gypsy, Spirit, Timber, nor I realized that we were in danger until Alistair McPherson walked into the clearing, holding a double barrel Remington 10-gauge coach gun leveled in my direction. The Highlander was alive and looked pissed, for his face bore the wounds of being peppered by the double-ought buck I had shot him with. It had always bothered me that they never found the outlaw's body after the shoot-out in Alma. Now, here he was, and he had the drop on me. I had no illusion of the outcome of this meeting. Alistair McPherson was here to kill me.

McPherson's smile was morbid and twisted from the wounds to his face as he spoke. "The tracks in the snow leading to the entrance of this hidden valley were almost a Godsend, but for the wind that was taking my scent away from you to let me come here from downwind was icing on the cake. It is time I finish this once and for all, Marshal. You have taken everything that I had worked for away from me. You, the wolf, and the friend you just said a sermon over killed my brother and all my men. I have no money, I have a limp, and my face is scarred for life because of you and that demon wolf of yours.

The air was now heavy with the tension of the moment and just as I felt that Alistair McPherson would pull the triggers of the coach gun, Timber sprinted not at McPherson which would have only been the death of the white wolf, but to the right of him.

This caused McPherson's plan of attack to be scattered and mistimed as he moved his shotgun from pointing at me toward the movement of Timber as he sprinted. McPherson instinctively pulled both triggers as I quickly palmed my Colt and fired three times as I fanned the hammer of my pistol. The first shot was lower as I gut-shot him just above his belt buckle. The second caught him higher up and in the center of his chest and a decent heart shot. The third caught him in the forehead above his right eye as his knees buckled as he was falling into the white virgin snow in front of him.

With the Highlander outlaw down and out and unmoving, I turned my attention to Timber, whose dash had saved both of our lives. Timber was moving as only he could, and it would seem that he had escaped any wounding or injury from being shot at from the Remington coach gun. Timber was now circling the body of McPherson as if he was checking for any signs of life. Loading my Colt before holstering it, I moved over and crouched down Indian style next to Timber and the now cooling body of the outlaw that finally got what he had coming to him for all the misery he had caused. I knew he was now at the gates of Hades waiting for his eternal damnation. With my arm over Timber, I looked into the eyes of the man I had just killed, and then I turned to Timber and looked in his eyes and said, "It would seem that my granddaughter knew all along that you would save my life on this trip. I'm thinking, my yellow-eyed friend, that you have earned a well-needed rest back home with Connor!"

Timber moved in closer, and he licked my face as if he was telling me he was ready to go home.

Kurt James

AUTHOR'S NOTE:

If you, the reader, have made it this far, that means you have finished reading my book "Connor's Saga," and I would just like to take a line or two to thank you for purchasing my work, and I hope you enjoyed the book.

It is my hope you have found Colorado to be a living and breathing character as much as Eric Robert, Connor, Matt Lee alias "Ghost" and of course Timber - I love Colorado and everything it offers.

You may ask - is the hidden valley named in the story Redemption Valley real? One thing I know is that Boreas Pass, in which the valley is located - I have in my life traveled numerous times, but to reveal if the valley is real would destroy the whole concept of "hidden." If you, the reader want to locate "Redemption Valley," you have enough clues in the story to locate it - if it is.

With maybe the exception of Redemption Valley, I want to assure you that the Colorado geography, along the path my heroes Eric Robert, Connor, Veronica, and Timber traveled through the Colorado Mountains, does in fact exist - every mountain, mountain range, mountain pass, town, mining camp, river, and creek.

I took some liberty in using the modern names in some cases or the more historical names if I thought it fit the story better. I wanted folks who were locals or familiar with this Colorado area to be able to follow along on Connor's Saga adventure more easily in their mind and to be able to travel if they wanted to on horseback, foot, or even by car or 4 wheel drive the same path of Matt Lee and Walk With Ghost as they tried to put their past behind them and find sanctuary in Redemption Valley.

The cover photo, as with my previous novels "Rocky Mountain Reckoning" and "Rocky Mountain Retribution" is one of my own taken in Rocky Mountain National Park.

ABOUT THE AUTHOR

Kurt James was born and raised in the foothills of the Colorado Rocky Mountains. With family roots in western Kansas and having lived in South Dakota for 20 years, Kurt James naturally has become an old western and nature enthusiast. Over the years Kurt James has become one of Colorado's prominent nature photographers through his brand name of Midnight Wind Photography. His poetry has been featured in the Denver Post, PM Magazine and on 9NEWS in Denver, Colorado. Kurt James' poetry is also featured at Creative Exiles, a collection of some of the finest poets on the web. Kurt James Reifschneider is also a feature writer for Hubpages with the articles focused on Colorado history, ghost towns, outlaws, and poetry. Inspired at a young age by writers such as Jack London, Louis L'amour and Max Brand, Kurt has formed his natural ability as a story teller. "Connor's Saga" is Kurt James' 6th novel and his 4th novel in his Rocky Mountain Series, but not the last novel of the western frontier of the wild and dangerous Colorado Rocky Mountains.

https://www.facebook.com/authorkurtjames/
http://hubpages.com/@kurtreifschneider
http://www.creativeexiles.com/author/kurtjames/
https://www.amazon.com/Kurt-James/e/B01DTOJ7KC/ref=dp_byline_cont_pop_ebooks_1

A sampling of Kurt James thrilling murder/mystery:

THE DAUNTING
BY
KURT JAMES

CHAPTER 18

Nickey Lynn, Gene and I, when we walked by Micah's missing poster, touched it as we walked out of the door. It was as if all of us had come together as one and were acting as a single person in the quest to find the answers to Craig Dale's disappearance and the others including my long lost best friend Micah. As we all got into our respective Grand County Sheriff's Blazers, I felt renewed in the sense that at least the sheriff's department and I seemed to be moving in the right direction in finding out what happened to Micah over four years ago.

The day matched my mood as there were zero clouds in the forever blue above my head. The sun was shining, and the wind had taken a vacation for now. The aspen trees dotting the mountainside were less golden color as autumn was making its final push toward the fast closing winter months. It would not be long and all the aspen leaves would be gone for the year. The Rocky Mountain seasons – as life – were a constant, never-ending cycle of rebirth and death. It was the same as it was when my Ute Indian ancestors and my famous Grandfather Matt Lee walked these mountains of old. This everlasting cycle of life and death spoke to the Indian side of me.

Nickey pulled out first, then Gene, and then myself as we headed eastward on Highway 40. Feeling good about the day, I popped a John Denver cassette into the player, and it was already fast forwarded to one of my favorite songs of his that reminded me of Micah, "Rocky Mountain High." "His sight has turned inside himself to try to understand…"

Following the Colorado River as it zigged and zagged along the highway, we made the west side of Granby and the Highway 34 junction in short order. We headed northbound toward Grand Lake which was where Nickey and Gene were heading to interview the park ranger Samael Amos and where I would continue on even further north into Rocky Mountain National Park to check on Craig Dale's Toyota Land Cruiser and speak to the park rangers there.

Passing Lake Granby on the east side of the road, I noticed that some ice had built up on the edges since the last time I had driven by here. There were several hardy fishermen along its shores enjoying the day. More fisherman were dotted along the shore of Shadow Mountain Lake as well. I thought that if Nickey and I had not been working, it would be a great day to fish.

Just past the general store and gas station on the highway was the road. We veered off east from Highway 34 that would become the West Portal Road and the main drag of Grand Lake Village that Nickey and Gene took as they now were heading into town. Passing that exit, I continued on north to Rocky Mountain National Park. Reaching down and grabbing the police radio microphone and pleased with myself for not dropping it, I depressed the send button and said, "Officer Chavez, make sure you take notes and see if Mr. Amos has any copies of anything he might have given Craig Dale in his research for his book."

There was a moment of silence before the radio crackled and Nickey responded, "Copy that, Undersheriff Lee."

Continuing north several miles, I came to the entrance of Rocky Mountain National Park that had several rangers working the booths and gates letting folks in once they paid or showed their yearly pass. Trail Ridge Road, the highest paved road in the world, would close in the next couple of weeks when the snow at those lofty heights would become unmanageable for the road crews. Trail Ridge always closed about the third week in October and would not reopen until the end of May the following year.

There were several cars at the crossing gates paying the fee and getting information for their day travels from the rangers as I pulled over to the side of the road. Cranking down my window halfway so I did not lock myself out, I left my county Blazer and the heater going to keep it warm when I stepped out into the crisp Rocky Mountain autumn air. I did not envy those that lived in Denver in what some locals here called the "Big Smoke" due to the ever present brown cloud that hovered over the city. I could not imagine having to breathe that smog of pollution that choked the city down there at the bottom of the foothills. Life here was cleaner and simpler. Just the way I liked it.

There were two rangers working the booths, and I knew both. Brett Hooper was in the class behind me in high school and we were friends and had gone fishing together several times although not in recent times. He was about six feet tall with blonde hair, a friendly sort with always a smile on his face. Sandee Adams was from Denver originally and was a very attractive petite blonde that had been a park ranger for over five years. I had dated Sandee casually up until I met Nickey Lynn, but we were still on friendly terms and knew each other well or about as well as those that had been intimate with each other.

All the cars that had been waiting to enter the park had paid their dues and had left, leaving the road abandoned for now. Since Sandee and Brett had a few minutes in between the tourists, they stepped out to greet me, Brett with a hardy handshake and Sandee with a small kiss on my cheek. Sandee spoke up first with a smile, "Well Dane, you are looking as handsome as ever and with the uniform and your six shooter, you must be here in an official capacity today. How is your lady doing?"

Sandee never called Nickey by name - it was always "your lady." Smiling, I said, "Nickey Lynn is doing fine and I will tell her you asked about her. As for the visit it is official; I came here to look at an abandoned Toyota Land Cruiser and a missing person case."

Brett spoke up in his official capacity as a park ranger and said, "The red one; we heard someone from your office would be here today. I will call ahead and get one of the rangers working the roads to come down and lead you to it. We had been keeping an eye on it and as one week turned into two weeks, we feared the worst."

Brett went back to his booth to make the call and left Sandee and me standing outside in the high mountain air when I asked her a question. "Do you know the park ranger Samael Amos?"

Sandee's smile evaporated, and she seemed to be in some deep thought before she replied, "Of course I do; he is one of our supervisors. Samael is like you Dane in some ways, and then not like you in other ways. He is very handsome and muscular and built like you, but taller. He spends all of his free time here in the park even during the winter months. He is a mountain climber and likes to explore the most remote areas of the park. He knows this park better than any man alive - that is for sure. He does his exploring all alone, and he told me once he was born 150-years too late and that he would have been the greatest mountain man of all time. Between you and me, he is an arrogant SOB. He looks at me and the others as we are just pieces of meat and we are beneath him because we do not take fitness as seriously as he does and that he thinks he is smarter than the rest of us. Other than that Dane, he is a nice enough fellow."

The last sentence was said with a chuckle, and it reminded me that Sandee was not only beautiful, but one hell of a woman. If I had not met Nickey, then I would probably still be with Sandee. Just as I was about to reply, five more cars showed up to enter the park, and Sandee smiled and said as she hurried to her booth, "Hold that thought, Dane."

Stepping quickly aside so the cars could pass, I wandered over and leaned against my Blazer as I waited for one of the field rangers to come down and show me where Craig Dale's red Toyota Land Cruiser was. I thought about what Sandee had said about Samael Amos, and I gathered he was not a likeable fellow by any means. And it seems he was a loner to boot. Thinking back to the first time I had read his name on the top of Craig Dale's list, I remembered what Nickey Lynn had told me about the name Samael. "That it was one of the Jewish myths, Samael was the grim reaper and a fallen angel. He is known as a destroyer and a seducer. He is also known by names like the Prince of Darkness and the chief of the Dragons of Evil."

Just as that thought ran its course through my mind, the police radio crackled and hissed until Nickey Lynn's voice came over the radio loud and clear, "OFFICER DOWN - ALL UNITS - OFFICER DOWN - NEED ASSISTANCE AND AMBULANCE ASAP 1220 3RD STREET, GRAND LAKE."

My mind went numb for a second as the radio went dead, and before my mind caught up to my body and I could move, the radio hissed and crackled again with the woman I loved in a voice that was losing its strength, "DANE - HURRY!"

www.ingramcontent.com/pod-product-compliance
Lightning Source LLC
Chambersburg PA
CBHW060217180626
46813CB00007B/2858